"You Know Common Sense Tells Me To Say No To You," Brianna Replied.

"I don't see that. You stand to gain a lot and lose very little unless you can't stand to be with me."

"You know full well there's no danger of any woman not being able to stand you," she said.

"Until this moment I was beginning to wonder. This is the coolest reception I've ever got."

He placed his hand on the car door, blocking her from opening it. Leaning closer, he lowered his voice. "I've asked you to be my wife tonight and we've never even kissed. That's a giant unknown when there's a marriage proposal between us."

Her pulse had raced all night, but now her heart thudded and she looked at his mouth. "I can remedy that one," she said, tingling at the thought of kissing him.

She moved in closer, stood on tiptoe and placed her lips on his.

His kiss might be her undoing.

Dear Reader,

Wyoming Wedding, the third book in the STETSONS &
CEOS trilogy, resolves the competition of Jared Dalton,
Chase Bennett and Matt Rome, three affluent cousins
who made a bet to see who could make the most money
during the year. Two cousins, Jared and Chase, have
been drawn north to their roots in South Dakota and
Montana. Ambitious and driven, Matt has opted to have
his headquarters in the state where he grew up, thus we
travel in this story to the third state, beautiful Wyoming.

Through his college years and shortly afterward,
Matt Rome, the tough former rodeo champion, parlayed
a bull-riding fortune into lucrative investments and
switched to a finance career. Now Matt needs a wife to
acquire more wealth and win the bet with his cousins.

What happens when two people who are poles apart in
their backgrounds—and are equally poles apart where
they're determined to go in their futures—find a hot
chemistry between them whenever they are together?
Sparks fly when they agree on a temporary paper
marriage that sizzles from the first night together. The
temporary marriage is merely a gambit to get what each
one wants, yet what happens after they have exchanged
vows? Read and see how the conflict spins out and
is resolved with the third CEO and the waitress he
discovers he can't resist.

Sara Orwig

SARA ORWIG

WYOMING WEDDING

Silhouette® Desire

Published by Silhouette Books

America's Publisher of Contemporary Romance

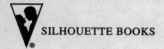 SILHOUETTE BOOKS

Recycling programs
for this product may
not exist in your area.

ISBN-13: 978-0-373-76947-6

WYOMING WEDDING

Copyright © 2009 by Sara Orwig

Visit Silhouette Books at www.eHarlequin.com

Printed in U.S.A.

Books by Sara Orwig

Silhouette Desire

Falcon's Lair #938
The Bride's Choice #1019
A Baby for Mommy #1060
Babes in Arms #1094
Her Torrid Temporary
  Marriage #1125
The Consummate Cowboy #1164
The Cowboy's Seductive
  Proposal #1192
World's Most Eligible Texan #1346
Cowboy's Secret Child #1368
The Playboy Meets His Match #1438
Cowboy's Special Woman #1449
††Do You Take This Enemy? #1476
††The Rancher, the Baby
  & the Nanny #1486

Entangled with a Texan #1547
*Shut Up and Kiss Me #1581
*Standing Outside the Fire #1594
Estate Affair #1657
†Pregnant with the First Heir #1752
†Revenge of the Second Son #1757
†Scandals from the Third Bride #1762
Seduced by the Wealthy Playboy #1813
‡Pregnant at the Wedding #1864
‡Seduced by the Enemy #1875
‡Wed to the Texan #1887
**Dakota Daddy #1936
**Montana Mistress #1941
**Wyoming Wedding #1947

††Stallion Pass
*Stallion Pass: Texas Knights
†The Wealthy Ransomes
‡Platinum Grooms
**Stetsons & CEOs

SARA ORWIG

lives in Oklahoma. She has a patient husband who will take her on research trips anywhere from big cities to old forts. She is an avid collector of Western history books. With a master's degree in English, Sara has written historical romance, mainstream fiction and contemporary romance. Books are beloved treasures that take Sara to magical worlds, and she loves both reading and writing them.

To David

One

October

Matt Rome sat in one of the best steak houses in Cheyenne, Wyoming. Waitpeople moved between linen-covered tables that held flickering candles. The dim lighting cast a spell over the room. The piano player explored an old tune. Having dined earlier with the woman from his most recent affair, Matt was back for a late-night coffee—on a mission. He'd tipped the maitre d' generously to seat him in the section assigned to Brianna Costin. While he watched her wait tables, hurrying between the dining room and kitchen, he ran his fingers along the handle of his coffee cup.

Whenever he saw her, it only served to reinforce his

opinion that she was one of the most beautiful women he'd ever seen. The fact that she was a waitress was no hindrance to his plans. Just the opposite—her status and income would probably make her more cooperative. She was tall with luscious curves and flawless skin. Her black hair was always thickly coiled at her nape. She suited his future plans fine.

His time and patience both had dwindled and still, he had no more likely a candidate for a paper marriage. Once, he would have given serious consideration to Nicole, the woman he'd had dinner with, but no longer. She was too demanding of his time. Their fight tonight had been the final push for them to break off relations. It had been easy to tell her goodbye when she'd issued an ultimatum to spend more time with her or get out of her life. His thoughts shifted to Brianna as she approached his table.

Usually his waitress now that he'd started requesting her, she was efficient and courteous. Beyond that, she seemed barely to take note of her patrons. Even though Matt always gave her impersonal courtesy—as if he hadn't noticed her, he couldn't avoid watching her as she made the rounds. Sometimes she would glance his way, whether out of professional reasons to keep up with her patrons' needs, or something more personal, he had no idea.

It was half an hour until closing, yet a few diners still lingered. Holding a carafe of coffee, Brianna approached his table to refill his cup.

"Do you want anything else?" she asked. Even

though she never held eye contact long, when he gazed into her thickly fringed green eyes, the contact fueled a primitive reaction.

"As a matter of fact, yes, I do," he replied. "I'm back to see you. I'd like to talk to you after work."

"I'm sorry. I never socialize with our patrons," she answered coolly, all friendliness leaving her voice. "It's better that way," she added without a flicker of change in her expression.

Unaccustomed to rejection, he bit back a smile. "I'm asking for an hour over a cup of coffee. If you prefer, you can meet me somewhere else. I promise you, I'm safe to be with," he said, reaching into his pocket to hand her a business card. "I'm Matt Rome."

"I know who you are," she replied. "I imagine everyone in Cheyenne knows who you are, Mr. Rome." Without glancing at the card, she pocketed it.

"It won't take long," Matt continued. "How's the Talon Club?" It was an expensive private club located at the top of one of the city's tallest buildings.

She smiled. "Thanks, but I don't believe they would allow me in—I'm not a member."

"I belong to the club. If you'll meet me in the lobby of the building, after your shift, they'll let us in. Or if you prefer, since it's three or four miles from your work, I can wait and follow you home to take you from your place."

As if mulling over his offer, she paused. "I have a feeling you intend to ask me something big. I can save you time by saying no now."

Again, he suppressed a smile. "This is not what

you're thinking, I can assure you. Here isn't the place to talk. I would wager a sizable bet you'll be pleased we talked tonight."

For the first time since he'd met her he seemed to have her full attention as her eyes narrowed a fraction. He waited, his amazement increasing. Matt could usually outlast any silence at a bargaining table, though as time stretched, he decided she was sticking by her refusal. "I understand you can't talk as freely here," he said finally.

"That's for sure. My clothes might not be presentable for the club either."

"Yes, they are," he said, glad to find she was considering his offer. She wore what every other waitperson in the restaurant wore—black slacks and a black shirt, only on her, the outfit was as stylish as a high-dollar ensemble.

"Very well, I'll meet you in the lobby at a quarter before midnight."

"Excellent," he said, his eagerness making him laugh at himself. When had it ever been this difficult to get a woman to go out with him? He was more amused than annoyed.

"You don't intend to order anything else now?" she asked.

He raised his coffee. "This is sufficient. As a matter of fact, I'll take the check so they can clear this table."

She left to return in a few minutes with his bill. "Thanks."

"I'll see you in the lobby," he said, and she was gone. Congratulating himself on his victory in getting her to go out, he watched her walk away. The black slacks rode low below her tiny waist that was emphasized by the ties of her white apron. He wondered how her legs looked— they were obviously long and slender. He liked watching her, mentally peeling away the slacks, wishing for a moment this was a restaurant where waitpeople wore skimpier clothing.

Despite the fact that she was reserved, and with obvious barriers, he remained interested.

Time seemed to drag in the lobby of the building that housed the club until the revolving door spun to reveal her. The apron was gone and her straight black hair cascaded over her shoulders. As she approached him, her hips swayed slightly. His desire stirred.

"I'm glad you came," he said, lust warming him.

"I'll reserve judgment on whether I can say the same or not."

He laughed. "I'll admit, the last woman who responded similarly was a little six-year-old girl in grade school, I think. I had some hostile encounters in the first grade," he said, expecting to wring a smile from her. Instead, she gave him another solemn glance and remained silent. "Let's have a drink and then we can talk," he said, motioning toward the dark, glossy elevators.

"Is this why you've asked for my section each time you've come to the dining room lately?" she probed as the elevator sped them skyward.

"Not exactly…maybe partially. You're good at your job."

"Thank you," she answered, giving him the feeling she was hoping to get this meeting over with so she could go home. Her lack of interest was beginning to bother him.

The maitre d' greeted them and escorted them to a table by the window overlooking the city. On the table, a small candle threw a soft glow on Brianna, catching shining glints in her silky dark hair. They gave their drink orders, hers a limeade and his a glass of brandy. As soon as they were alone, she looked at him expectantly.

"I've wanted to meet you," he said, and something flickered in her eyes that made him suspect that she felt the sparks as much as he did. That awareness jolted him.

"Brianna, I've had my staff look into your background so I could learn more about you," he said. This time the flash in her green eyes was unmistakable indignation.

"I'd call that an invasion of my privacy."

"Not really. I only have information that is more or less public knowledge. You're from Blakely, Wyoming, the first of your family to attend college. You're enrolled in Wyoming University in Laramie, commuting from Cheyenne—that one stumped me even though it isn't a long drive."

"I doubt if it gave the information that I found a better job here and I only have classes on campus on Tuesdays and Thursdays this semester, thanks to the convenience of online classes. So tell me what else you know about me."

"You have five siblings, two married sisters and three younger brothers. One brother is still in high school and all three of them work. You are a senior in college and you hope to go to law school."

"So far, you're right. How much deeper did you look into my private life? Do you do this with every woman you invite out?"

"Calm down," he said, noticing her words were becoming more clipped. Her irritation was showing.

"How's school going?"

"I have a suspicion you already know. I like my classes. So far, I have all A's."

"Commendable," he remarked. "And at the moment there is no man in your life. I'm surprised there wasn't one waiting in the wings. You're a beautiful woman."

"Thanks, and there isn't one, waiting or otherwise," she said with the first faint smile since her arrival.

"What do you really enjoy? Tell me about yourself," he said, leaning back slightly.

"I have the feeling I'm being interviewed for something," she said. "I like cold winter nights, roaring fires, roasting marshmallows. I like achieving my goals, living in the city." As she talked, he watched her. They were the closest face-to-face they had ever been, and she was even more gorgeous up close. Her green eyes captivated him, and he could only imagine them filled with passion. Her bow-shaped mouth and full lips made it impossible to avoid conjuring up fantasies of kissing her. She was composed, rarely gesturing when she talked with a soft voice that was as sexy as everything else about her.

"And what do you dream about doing?" he asked,

trying to get through the barrier she kept between them. For some reason, probably out of her past, she had a chip on her shoulder. Or perhaps it was because any man with a pulse would try to hit on her. He knew she had men in her life on occasion.

"I dream about being a lawyer, having complete independence, helping my family."

"But on a more personal level? Everybody has hopes and longings."

"That's easy," she replied, smiling at him. "I want to see things I've never seen in real life—palm trees, seashells, the ocean, tropics with balmy weather. I've never seen the ocean. Actually, I've never been out of Wyoming or even flown in a plane." For the first time, she looked as if she had relaxed with him. "I dream about going to Europe because pictures of foreign places are breathtaking. So, Mr. Rome, what do you dream of doing when you've probably already done everything in life you want to do?"

"It's Matt, not Mr. Rome. What do I want? That's part of what this is about," he said, pausing when their drinks were served. "I hope what I'm going to discuss is something appealing, not something threatening to you."

"Since we've been all around the mulberry bush, so to speak, why don't you tell me why I'm here?"

"I'm not certain being so direct is going to help you in law school," he observed.

"I'm not in law school tonight," she said, and he knew she was waiting for an answer to her question.

"This evening isn't going exactly the way I expected.

I'll grant that while I don't know you, I'd like to. Will you have dinner with me tomorrow night?"

When she stared at him in silence, he thought perhaps she was going to get up and walk out. "You could have asked me that when I was your waitress at dinner. It didn't take all this."

"I want to get to know you. Also, I had a feeling if I'd asked you then, you would have turned me down."

"You're right. I think there's more to this than going to dinner with you. Guys at the club ask me out often and they don't actually take me out ahead of time to do so."

"Let me guess—you've never gone out with any of them."

"You're right," she said. "You and the other men who ask me out want one thing—my body. I'm not in your social class and we both know that. I'm a waitress, you're a wealthy bachelor. Not all the men who've asked me out are even single. I've received explicit invitations when the wife is in the powder room. At least you're not married."

As she looked away, her cheeks flushed a bright pink. The color heightened her beauty, and he knew he wanted her body as much as any other man had. Every inch of her was enticing. So far, he also enjoyed being with her—all reasons to support the argument that he was making an acceptable decision.

Zach Gentner's warning floated in the back of his mind. He could recall too clearly his best friend and chief investment advisor trying to talk him out of even thinking about getting to know her. Zach had his own arguments:

her poverty-stricken background, her lack of education, her lower-class life, her large, uneducated family.

Worst of all, she was three or four weeks pregnant by a man who had run out on her. That last argument had almost carried the day for Zach, until the next time Matt had gone to the club to eat. With Nicole accompanying him, he had surreptitiously watched Brianna, finding he was still drawn to her. Because of her pregnancy she might possibly be an even more likely candidate. She would need the money—no other woman on his list of candidates did. Until Brianna, the women he had taken out since college had been almost as wealthy or wealthier than he was. He knew, too, without any doubts, that all the other women on his list, including Nicole Doyle, would not want a two-year marriage of convenience. Not at all. He and Nicole had fought tonight over how seldom she had seen him. He was tired of her relentless dissatisfaction, which made him leery of choosing her as a candidate for his proposal.

Brianna seemed the perfect choice and when the marriage ended, she would be easier to get out of his life.

Leaning forward, she propped her chin on her fist and seemed to shake off the anger in her previous comment as she smiled at him. "So again, Matt, what's behind all this really?" Brianna inquired in a coaxing voice.

Desire flared. He wondered if lust had completely clouded his judgment as Zach had declared. Perhaps it had, because at the moment, Matt knew he craved her with an intensity that surprised him.

"All right, I'll get to the point. First hear me out. I'm

going to present something to you. Before you give me an answer, I want you to think about it for at least twenty-four hours or even several days if you want. Will you agree to that?"

As disappointment took the smile off her face, she sat up straight, all of her barriers once again in place with a frosty chill settling around her. "I think I can give you an answer right now. It's definitely not."

"You're jumping to conclusions. I'm not going to ask you to be my mistress."

Her eyes widened in surprise. "I can't imagine one other possibility you'd have for wanting to talk to me. I don't have any skills or a degree, so you're not out to hire me. What *do* you want?" Now she was filled with obvious curiosity, and he was satisfied that he finally had her full attention. The first little nagging doubts tugged at him that he might be making a mistake, only not for the reasons Zach had given. Matt didn't care about her background because she could rise above that and, as his wife, she would be accepted. What worried him for the first time was finding out that she had a strong will and a stubborn streak. Sticking with his decision, he pushed away worries.

He took her hand in his. The first physical contact startled him. He was going to make a commitment. "I need a wife. I want a marriage of convenience."

Two

Shock came first. A marriage proposal from Matt Rome, probably the wealthiest man in Wyoming, a man she knew only because she was his *waitress.* Her second thought was—as his wife, she would have money. Real money, oodles of money.

A mansion and a sports car and no more struggling to put food on the table—her head spun. At the same time she was filled with disbelief. She turned icy and alternately awash in heat.

Then common sense set in. Billionaires did not propose marriage to her. Actually, only Tommy Grogan at home had ever proposed and that had been when she was sixteen years old. She knew, down to her toes, that there was a catch to this offer and it must be a whopper.

All her defenses rushed back and she was ready to end the evening and go home in spite of her promise to hear him out. Reeling from it or not, she suspected if she knew the full story, she wouldn't want any part of what he had on his mind.

"Why me?" she asked. "You have beautiful women in your life from the same kind of society background. Why are you asking me instead of one of them?"

"That's your opinion, not mine. For one thing, they bore me. For another, I want this marriage for a short time, two years max. Then I want to be able to dissolve it without an emotional hassle and walk away. I think that will be much easier to do with you than with one of them," he added dryly. The latter reason made sense to her.

"Any other explanations why you chose me?" she asked, knowing that when he found out about her secret pregnancy, he would withdraw his offer. That alone was justification for him to find a more likely candidate for his marriage proposal.

"Why do you want this?" she asked, knowing there had to be something behind his proposal.

"There's an international investment group of men I want to join. I have a couple of friends in it. I'm a likely candidate except for being a bachelor. They're concerned about a bachelor's lifestyle, even though mine is far from wild. If I marry, they'll view me as settled."

She had mixed feelings: caution vied with temptation. She couldn't imagine it was as simple as he presented, yet he was bound to reward her generously. Two years as Matt Rome's wife? The thought made her giddy. Dreading telling him about her pregnancy, she knew she should end this.

"Why would you want to be in the group? You're enormously successful now. You don't need money."

When he smiled, her heart skipped. He was irresistibly handsome with his curly black hair and thick lashes that emphasized his clear blue eyes. She, along with all the other females in the vicinity, had always noticed him when he'd come to the dining room where she worked. Fortunately, she'd never made an issue of it and he didn't seem aware of her reaction to him. She'd heard everyone talk. In a club filled with wealthy members, Matt Rome stood out because he was the richest. And probably the youngest. He was hands-down the best-looking, with a smile to die for.

He had seemed attentive to the different women he brought to the steak house, although she knew earlier he and the woman with him had had a heated, drawn-out disagreement.

"I'd like to get into the group because they're far more successful than I've been. They're international and will open doors for me that won't be opened otherwise. I'll make more money faster."

"You have more money than you can spend. Why would you want to make more?" she persisted, and his blue eyes twinkled with amusement.

"Maybe it's the challenge of making it. There's never such a thing as too much money," he added as she shook her head.

"I can't imagine wealth like yours. If I had that much, I think I'd want to quit striving for more."

"You'll see someday. If you become a successful lawyer, you'll want more money."

"That wouldn't bring me anywhere close to your wealth." She sipped her limeade and put it down. "You don't want me. Even if you may have checked me out, there's a very big reason you will want to look elsewhere."

"Your pregnancy?" he asked.

She stared at him for a moment, at a loss for words. "I thought medical records were private."

"They are. There are other ways to find out."

"One of my friends must have talked," she said, narrowing her eyes and remembering only two of her closest friends, plus the father, had been told what she thought had been her secret. "I suppose once you tell someone, it's no longer a secret."

"A pregnancy is something you can hide for only so long. It might actually be a plus. I understand you're not very far along."

She shook her head, amazed by all he'd learned about her. "No, I went to the doctor two weeks ago and found out. I'm barely a full month."

"It definitely doesn't show," he said.

"No, not yet."

"What about the father?"

"He's out of my life. He's gone and he left no forwarding address, so to speak—which suited me. He legally signed away all privileges and rights." She continued, "He came from a big family and he never wanted kids. Actually, he turned out to be a jerk. He is on a full scholarship, so he's intelligent, which may be a good biological trait for the baby. But he and I didn't part on the best of terms," she answered, giving Matt the same information she'd told her two closest friends. She'd been devastated when the doctor told her she was pregnant. One of her friends had had a party and she remembered how much fun she'd had that night with a guy she saw there and had known from school. She tried to focus on what Matt was saying to her, looking at his blue eyes, eyes the color of the Wyoming sky on a clear summer day. She knew she had to get away from his influence, to think over his proposal with a clear head.

"You've told me what you'll get out of this marriage of convenience. What will I get from the union?"

He smiled, that captivating smile that had probably set too many female hearts fluttering. He was handsome. Handsome and rich beyond dreams. "You'll get half a million dollars when we marry, the other half when we divorce."

"A million dollars!" She gasped. She stared at him, unable to imagine having such money.

"That's right," he confirmed his statement.

"And a divorce later—won't they boot you out if you divorce?"

"They have two men who have divorced and the group let them remain, so I think I can weather that scandal. We'll keep a divorce low-key. I'm willing to take the risk to get this marriage and join the group."

"You expect to get your way, don't you?"

"Why not?" He smiled at her, conveying a cocky self-assurance. "Now back to discussing what you get out of this union. In addition," he continued, "I'll take care of the expenses of your pregnancy and the baby's birth. I'll give you a weekly allowance of a thousand dollars, that's yours for however you wish to spend it. You can buy a new car with my approval of your selection. It's yours when we part. You can get a new wardrobe now with my approval—no mink coat at this point. I want a real marriage as far as sex is concerned and I want you to move in with me."

In spite of trying, she couldn't stifle her laugh. He cocked one dark eyebrow as he surveyed her with curiosity. "You don't know me—you may not be able to stand me after I move in with you," she said. The money kept dangling in her thoughts. A million dollars for her!

"We're doing all right so far. Granted, the past hour has been a little cut-and-dried. But don't worry, I'll move you out if I don't like it," he replied.

She shook her head. "You must want in this group desperately."

His amusement vanished. "Joining this investment bunch is important and I intend to get an invitation from them. If it means I have to marry to do so, so be it."

"I can't imagine any amount of money making it worthwhile to get locked into a loveless marriage."

"That's why you're the perfect selection for me," he said, leaning forward to grasp her hand. "You're gorgeous," he said, and her pulse jumped to a faster speed.

"You're intelligent. You're sexy. You work hard. You're honest."

"You don't know that at all. Sorry, I guess that didn't sound so good on my part," she added hastily and knew her face flushed in embarrassment. "There has to be something to this besides more money."

"No, there isn't. Money is enough."

"Then why the rush? Why don't you wait? In another few months you might fall in love. Why rush into a paper marriage?"

"I'm in a rush because my two cousins and I have a bet that ends next May. It's to see which one of us can make the most money before that May deadline. I want to win the bet. If I join this group, I think I can."

"All this is over a bet?" she asked in disbelief, beginning to wonder if he was as smart as she'd heard and read. "No bet is worth getting married for."

"Ahh, this one might be. I'll win that bet, I think, if I join this group."

"Then it must be for an enormous prize. How much money is at stake?"

"We each put in five million dollars. In May winner gets all and the winner treats for a weekend getaway where we can all be together."

"Five million each!" she echoed. She had always heard about his wealth, to actually deal with it left her dismayed. She counted pennies. He didn't even count thousands. "That's astounding you toss money around like that."

"It isn't exactly tossing. I intend to win, I promise you."

"You're driven," she declared, staring at him and wondering about his life that seemed totally focused on making money.

"The pot is calling the kettle black. You're ambitious yourself."

"On a tiny scale compared to you. And our reasons are light-years apart. My goals are meant to get me out of a life of poverty. Your goals are to achieve a whim."

She smiled to take the edge off her statement, feeling sparks ignite between them. He certainly knew how to charm women.

"How do those terms sound to you?" he asked.

"Like a dream. They don't seem real to me. I've never even been alone with you until we came here," she said.

"So far, so good, I'd say. I'm enjoying the moment."

"To my surprise, I am, too," she said. "How could I not enjoy being proposed to and offered so much money?" she asked and they both smiled.

"It has happened, though. I want you to think about it for a few days."

"Where will I live if I marry you?" she asked, thinking the moment was turning surreal.

"I live here in Cheyenne. I have other homes and I have a ranch near Jackson Hole. Does it matter?"

"Not really. When I finish school, I had expected to move out of state to get a job. Now I'll stay near my family because of my baby."

"You may want to rethink your future. If you marry me and I pay you a million, you won't need degrees. I don't want you laboring over college texts when I need you at my side for parties and travel."

She pursed her lips and ran her finger along her cold, empty glass as she shook her head. "That's a problem because I don't want to give up my education. I can take classes in the mornings when you're at work. Also, I can juggle things and make arrangements with professors to make up the work when we travel."

Now he sat in silence, turning his empty brandy glass in his fingers. He had well-shaped hands, broad shoulders and she knew enough from newspapers that he had once been a champion bull rider. Beneath the slick billionaire façade was a tough cowboy, she suspected and guessed that was why he'd kept the family ranch and still remained based in Wyoming.

Feeling their clash of wills, she wondered how often they would disagree. Even if it would be easier to get her out of his life, he was taking a huge chance by asking her to marry him when he didn't know her.

"I was thinking," she voiced her thoughts aloud, "you'd be better off marrying someone in love with you because she'd do everything you want to try to keep you happy."

"If we agree to this marriage, I think we'll work out our differences," he said, and she could detect the supreme confidence in his tone.

"If this marriage is for two years, you'll have a baby on your hands," she reminded him.

"With my money, I don't see that as a problem. I'd claim your baby as mine as far as the public is concerned. That will make me appear even more settled and reliable to this investment group."

Her indignation flared—he would view her baby merely as a means to achieve his end he wanted. She bit back a retort because she wanted to think about possibilities. He wanted to look married and settled and respectable. Reliable. That might give her leverage for bargaining for more for her baby.

"I can see the wheels turning in your head," he said, looking mildly amused. "What do you want?"

"I'm thinking about what you just told me. You'll look terrible if you walk out on a wife and baby."

"So I will, but I'll probably get some sympathy if you walk out on me and take the baby, leaving me because of the long hours I work."

She shook her head. "I suppose that would bring you some sympathy, especially from men who work as long and hard as you."

"So this all looks viable to you?"

"I'm torn between walking out right now or staying and giving consideration to your proposal. It's the coldest, most hard-hearted marriage proposal ever. On the other hand, you know I need what you're offering."

"So you'll think it over?" he asked.

"Of course I will. In some ways, it's the opportunity of a lifetime."

"Maybe if we can get past the proposal, we can find we're good company for each other. Sooner or later, I would have gotten to know you anyway."

She smiled at him. "I find that one a real stretch. I

don't think I would have been in your future if you hadn't needed this."

"We'll see how it goes between us." He leaned forward and reached across the table. "Let's let it go for now. You can mull it over later."

She glanced at her watch, looking up at him in surprise. "It's after one! We need to get out of here so they can close."

"The club is open until two," he said, coming around to hold her chair. "You need your sleep for the baby. We should go." He walked with her out to her car. "I'll follow you home. It's late."

"I drive alone all the time. It's a wonder I survived before I met you."

"I'll follow you," he said in a tone that ended her argument. He put his hand on the car door to stop her from opening it and she looked up at him.

"Tomorrow night, would you prefer to go out to eat, or to eat at my place where we can have a little more privacy to discuss my proposal? You can see where you might live soon."

"I can't believe this is actually happening to me."

"You'll believe it before long."

"Can I look up anything about this investment group you want to get into?"

"Yes." He pulled a card out of his pocket and wrote on the back of it. "Here are some names. Start with these. This group is real."

"I'm sure it's real. I want to know about it."

"I'll pick you up tomorrow night about seven."

"You know common sense tells me to say no to you."

"I don't see that. You stand to gain a lot and lose very little unless you hate being with me."

"You know full well there isn't a female on this earth whose heartbeat doesn't speed up when you're around, so there's no danger of any woman not being able to stand being with you," she said.

"Until this moment, I was beginning to wonder about you. This is the coolest reception in my adult life."

He stretched his arm out again, placing his hand on her car door and blocking her from opening it. Leaning closer, he lowered his voice. "I've proposed to you tonight and we've never even kissed. That's a giant unknown when there's a marriage proposal."

While her pulse had raced all night, now her heart thudded and she looked at his mouth. "I can remedy that one," she said, tingling at the thought of kissing him. She stepped closer to slide her arm around his shoulders, feeling the soft wool of his suit jacket and beneath it, the warmth of his body.

She moved even closer, stood on tiptoe and placed her lips on his. She had started the kiss as if she were tackling a math problem, yet the moment his tongue slid into her mouth, the kiss changed. Heat suffused her, spiraling down to pool low within her and build a fire of physical longing that burned with scorching flames.

His arm banded her waist, pulling her tightly against him, his fingers tangling in her long hair. He leaned over her, his tongue thrusting deep and exploring slowly, a hot, sexy kiss that intensified desire. She would never again be able to view him as dispassionately as she had prior to this moment. His kiss was melting her, stirring longing for so much more with him, surprising her because never had any man's kisses affected her the way Matt's did.

His fiery kiss made his proposal infinitely more inviting. She suspected she wouldn't think straight in the next few minutes about any decisions.

How long they kissed she didn't know. She ran her fingers through his hair, down the strong column of his neck. His tight embrace pressed his arousal against her, hard and ready.

It was late; the restaurant would close and other patrons would come out into the parking lot. She and Matt weren't kissing in a private place. All the dim arguments nagged, though they were faint inducements to stop.

Her pulse roared and she wanted to unbutton his shirt and place her hands on his chest. Realizing what she was about to do, she gathered her wits and pushed lightly against his chest instead.

Pausing, he raised his head as they both gasped for breath.

"Marry me, Brianna," he said and she opened her mouth to answer. Instantly he shook his head and put his finger on her lips. He seemed to pull himself together.

"Don't rush an answer. Your kiss made me ask you again," he said, his blue eyes focused intently on her with a searching look as if he, too, had been surprised by his reaction to their kiss.

She hoped he had been. She didn't want to fade into

the long line of women in his life—all of whom he seemed able to ignore and get rid of sooner or later. In that moment, she knew if she accepted his offer, she would have to guard her heart with all her being to escape falling in love with him.

Moving his hand away, he took her keys to open her car door, holding it for her before returning the keys. As soon as she slid behind the wheel, he closed the door and leaned down as she lowered the window. "Go to dinner with me tomorrow night."

"Of course I will."

"Thanks for meeting with me tonight. I know you didn't want to when I asked you at the restaurant."

"It's been interesting, to say the least. I'll go home and think over your proposal and see you tomorrow night."

"Sure," he said, stepping back away from the car and heading to his own. Turning on the ignition, she drove out without waiting for him. In minutes when she glanced into the rearview mirror, beneath streetlights she saw him following behind her in his sleek gray Jaguar. She drove to the old apartments that were near her work. She parked in the graveled lot and hurried to the side door, turning to wave at him as he waited nearby in the parking lot where he could see her go inside.

Smells of old fast-food boxes and mildew permeated the halls, the sour odor a permanent one. Climbing the steps to the second floor, she entered her apartment that was on the front of the complex. She shared a cramped two-bedroom apartment with Faith Wellston, one of her closest friends and a classmate.

As she shed her clothes and pulled on a heavy nightgown, she considered Matt's proposal. She assessed her surroundings and wondered how she could question the answer she would give him. He was sexy, handsome and appealing. Yet, from all he had said, money was his first love. Maybe his only love. He was going into a paper marriage that, except for sex, was a coldhearted business deal. Yet what difference should that make to her?

His proposal included sex. After his kiss, the mere thought of sex with him made her temperature soar. She shoved aside a stack of textbooks and papers on the scarred kitchen table and pulled out a blank sheet of paper, drawing two columns to represent the pros and cons of accepting his proposal.

His love of money was number one on her con list. And the only thing on the con side. The pro side, she could fill the page. She heard a key turn in the door and Faith walked in.

"Studying this late? Quiz tomorrow?" Faith asked, raking her fingers through her thick red curls.

"Nope. Did you have fun tonight?"

Faith tossed down a stack of textbooks and her purse, then headed for the fridge, her flip-flops flapping with each step. She leaned over to get a cold bottle of water and wiped it on the tail of her gray T-shirt before coming back to the table to pull out a chair and sit facing Brianna. "No, I didn't have any fun tonight. Cal and I went to the library and studied for an exam we have Friday. So what did you do?"

"You wouldn't guess if I gave you all night," Brianna

said. The excitement that she'd tried to stifle all evening made her wiggle and grin. "Ever heard of Matt Rome?"

"Sure. You've said he comes to the restaurant." Faith narrowed her light brown eyes. "He hit on you?"

"Oh, no. Better than that. He wanted me to meet him after work."

"Wow!" Faith let out a squeal and sat up in the chair. "Tell me about it. So he wants to take you out again?"

"Yes, he does, only there's more—a two-year marriage of convenience!" she announced, excitement bubbling up as she threw the paper in the air.

"Marry him! You've got it made! The baby will be paid for and provided for completely," Faith cried. Springing up, she pulled on Brianna and they both danced wildly for a few minutes, Brianna enjoying the moment and letting go all the restraint she'd struggled to exhibit with Matt.

When Faith sat finally, she leaned forward. "How soon? He must be paying you."

"He's made me an offer and told me to think about it before I give him an answer."

"So how much?"

"Half a million now and the other half when we divorce. And we will divorce."

Faith screamed again, throwing up her hands. "A million dollars! Why didn't you accept tonight?" Instantly, her smile vanished. "Did you tell him about the baby?"

"Yes, I did, although he already knew, Faith, from someone," Brianna said, staring hard at Faith, whose eyes widened.

"Not from me." She raised her hand. "I swear, I haven't told anyone with the exception of Cal and he promised to keep quiet. I'll ask him if he talked to anyone."

"It doesn't matter so much now. Matt knows about it and is okay with it."

"Why does he want a paper marriage?" Faith asked.

"Now you're getting to the point. I'm making a list and giving my reply some thought," she said, retrieving the list she had started and waved it at Faith. "My pros and cons list. His life revolves around him acquiring more money all the time. He wants an in to some international investment group and they're leery of letting in a bachelor, hence the marriage."

"That's okay," Faith said, seeming to think about it.

"Maybe. I think his attitude is cold and hard-hearted and material."

"So what are you? You're as driven as anyone I've ever seen and you want your education with a vengeance. The only reason you had a one-night stand was because you finally let your hair down and had too many drinks and had some fun."

"And accidentally got pregnant," Brianna said.

Faith grabbed the pro and con sheet and ripped it in half. "Marry him and stop even thinking about pros and cons. I've seen the guy—he's gorgeous. All of us in Advanced Statistics got to go to a seminar where he was on the panel. He was engaging and magnetic. He's the most moneyed man in Wyoming, maybe. How could you possibly bicker about that? Two years—spectacular. Marry him, use the money and your life will never be the same. It'll mean care for your baby, no worries for you and all the education you want. You'll get out of the dumps like this," she said without pausing. "Forget arguments. Go for it. I would have said yes on the spot."

"I started to and he stopped me and said to think it over."

Faith snorted, puffing out her cheeks. "What's to think over? If he had a kinky lifestyle, it would have already been in the news, so no problem there. Say yes tomorrow night. What'll you wear? Let's go see."

The following night Brianna was all nerves. Faith had already left the apartment. Taking quick breaths to calm down, Brianna walked to the mirror to look again at her image. Studying her plain, black cotton dress, she recalled the few clothes she'd brought with her when she'd graduated from high school and arrived in Cheyenne with a scholarship to college. She'd had few clothes. One formal dress that was bright blue and yellow, several pairs of worn jeans, flip-flops, T-shirts, one plain brown skirt and one white cotton blouse that she'd worn to job interviews. She wondered how many details of her past Matt knew—if he'd known she'd gotten the job at the ritzy steak house in her junior year. No one could know except Faith, whom she'd told, how she'd studied the female patrons to notice their clothing and she began to change her home wardrobe accordingly. While she assumed Matt would find her clothes too cheap, at least she knew they weren't tacky.

When the doorbell buzzed, she grabbed up her purse and her list of what she wanted if they married. Glancing at it one more time, her heart raced. Would this list cause him to revoke his marriage offer? That's what Faith feared, but Brianna kept telling herself to stick by what she wanted. Matt Rome needed this marriage. Now she'd see how badly.

Three

When she opened the door, the first thing she saw was a smile that made her knees weak. How could she argue with Matt over anything? She wondered if he had a clue about the dreams that now filled her life.

"Hi," he said. "You look great."

"Thank you," she replied. "I'm ready. You can come in if you want. I'll warn you, my place is pretty plain."

"If you're ready, we'll go," he answered easily. His charcoal suit jacket was unbuttoned and while dressed for something fancy this evening, there was an aura of earthy sexuality about him that his suit couldn't tame.

After she locked her door, he took her arm to walk with her to his car, holding the door until she slid inside. As she watched him circle the front of the car, she

slipped her hand over the luxurious tan leather uphol-
stery. The Jaguar's walnut paneling in the interior had a
beautiful sheen and she marveled at the world of money.
This was the most elegant car she'd ever ridden in.

Yet she couldn't shake Faith's warnings. Faith had told
her repeatedly not to make demands on Matt, to accept
what he had offered and enjoy life because it was far
better than she would ever see otherwise. Too true, except
she had no doubt he could afford what she was asking.

As she watched him walk in front of the car, her concerns of money and needs and marriage ebbed. Wind
caught dark locks of his hair, blowing them away from
his forehead. He was incredibly handsome. Her heart
pounded and she remembered their passionate kiss that
had filled her with longing. They would be together all
the rest of the evening. The excitement made her bubbly.
She knew she should get her feelings under control so she
could think clearly. She was the only advocate she had.

As he sat behind the wheel, he glanced at her. "Ready?"

"Of course," she answered, smiling. "Drive me to
dinner in the most opulent car I've ever ridden in."

He laughed. "We're going back to the club—the main
dining room tonight. They have good food, only where
you work is one of the best restaurants in the state."

"That's good to hear from a customer."

"Have you thought about my proposal?"

"I haven't been able to think about anything else," she
admitted. "When I went to classes today, I gave up my
front-row seat in each of them to sit at the back because
I knew I wouldn't hear one word of the lecture anyway."

"I'm glad to know you're thinking about it."

"My friend is blown away by it."

"And I take it you're not," he said, smiling. There was speculation in his gaze as he glanced at her.

"We can talk about it when you're not driving. I need your full, undivided attention. In the meantime, tell me about your day."

"Today was mostly business as usual." While he talked about projects and investments, she gazed at him, thinking she could look endlessly at him. She still couldn't believe what was happening to her. It was a Cinderella story, only the prince was in love with money and she was merely the means to an end. Still, there were such promising prizes for her—she would be worth a million dollars. She couldn't get that out of her thoughts and again, the list in her hand was a fiery torch. She didn't want to get burned by it.

Soon he was relating funny anecdotes, and she relaxed slightly, despite the electric current bubbling in her since she first sat to talk to him last night.

When they walked into the darkened dining room of the downtown club, she wanted to pinch herself to know it was all real. She never had evenings like this and she knew she would remember every detail for the rest of her life. A pianist sang the lyrics to the slow song he played while several couples already circled the small dance floor.

They chose a martini for him and milk for her after they were seated. As he gazed at her, the flickering glow of the candles highlighted his prominent cheekbones. He reached over to hold her hand. "Let's dance."

She walked to the dance floor to step into his arms, and it sent her pulse into overdrive. His legs brushed hers lightly, and every touch stirred a riveting response. Just as his car had been an extension of his fortune, she was aware of everything else that proclaimed his wealth—from his fine wool suit to his inviting aftershave, something men she'd known had seldom worn.

She knew she had to accept his proposal. As fast as that thought occurred, she reminded herself to hold out for her most important demands. When he heard her requests, would he get angry? Could she fit into his world of power and money? So many questions about a future which had spun off into the unknown.

"You're deep in thought tonight," he said, his voice quiet as he held her close to slow dance.

"I'm wondering if I can ever get accustomed to things you take for granted. I've never ridden in a car like yours before. I don't have the table manners or the background to go the places you'll go."

"You'll learn. It won't be a problem, I promise. And my world is filled with regular people, the same as your world."

"Our environments aren't the same at all," she said, thinking now more about their kiss last night. She looked at his mouth, a slightly full lower lip. Two years and then marriage to him would be over. One thing she was absolutely certain about—life in the future would be all new to her and she should avoid ever trying to make him the center of it.

"So what else is on your mind?" he asked, watching her intently.

"I'm still thinking about your proposal," she answered.

"Good. That's what I wanted you to do," he said.

When the music changed to a fast number and couples melted away around them, Matt continued to hold her hand. "Let's keep going."

As she watched his cool moves, she forgot contracts, bargaining and wealth. All she could think about was Matt and how attractive he was. She wanted to kiss him again, wanted him to kiss her. Every move of his was sensual, heating her and causing erotic fantasies, images she tried to banish.

Tossing her head, she circled around him and then met his gaze and she knew he wanted her in his arms. If they had been alone, she thought, by now they would have been in an embrace.

There would be no problems with the physical part of their relationship. She worried about her requests for more money and wondered if she should abandon her demands.

When the song ended, he took her hand to return to their table. A couple approached them from Matt's side and he paused. Brianna stopped to wait and recognized a woman Matt had brought to the steak house in the past. The tall, slender blonde glanced at Brianna and then turned her attention to Matt. She was stunning in an intricately embroidered and beaded black dress and the tall man with her was almost as handsome as Matt. They stopped and the men shook hands, exchanging greetings.

"We're leaving," the tall, black-haired man said.

"Nicole, Ty, this is Brianna Costin. Brianna, this is Nicole Doyle and Ty Bookman."

"I barely recognized you out of your waitress uniform," Nicole said acidly to Brianna. "I believe we already know each other. You work at the steak house, right?"

"Yes, I do," Brianna answered.

"The food here is almost as delicious as it is there," Nicole added, turning to Matt. "We've eaten and are going. It's good to see you again, Matt," she said in a warmer tone.

Ty echoed her greeting and they moved on.

"Ignore her, Brianna."

"She didn't say anything that isn't so, although if looks could kill, I'd be a goner."

"There's nothing between us. Nicole is out of my life," he said, holding Brianna's chair for her.

He sat facing her again, opening his jacket. Dark locks of hair had fallen on his forehead and he looked more appealing than when he was buttoned up with every hair combed into place.

"That was better. You're more relaxed tonight. Last night, I felt as if I were standing outside castle walls with the drawbridge up."

She laughed. "If you're comparing me to a princess in a castle, that's a first. No one has ever drawn that comparison. Cinderella in ashes wouldn't be as wild an exaggeration. I came from nothing. My sisters and I all shared one room."

"Are they all as pretty as you?"

"I don't know about that. We resemble each other and

look like my mother, thank heavens. My brothers look like my dad, who was a charming man, merely unfaithful and unreliable and unable to hold a job. Actually, I don't think my dad liked to work."

"Some people don't. Evidently, he stayed inside the law, so that's commendable."

"Yes, he did as far as anyone ever knew. He liked bars and women. I wasn't getting into that trap. My sisters married early and young. I got scholarships. When I got to Cheyenne I got part-time jobs and here I am."

"I've noticed you since the first time I ever saw you at the steak house. It was a June night last year and I ate on the terrace and I don't even remember who I ate with."

"You remember that?" she asked, feeling her face flush and her pulse jump because she couldn't imagine him noticing and remembering a waitress. "Actually, I remember the night. I was new on the job. When I was assigned to your table, one of the other waitresses who had befriended me gave me the scoop."

"What did she tell you? Not that I'm demanding, I hope."

"Of course not. Not to me anyway," she said, and he smiled.

"You've never given me any indication that you've noticed me more than you do the busboys or the maitre d' or anyone else there. Had I but known," she said, fanning herself and teasing him, getting another smile from him.

She kept waiting all through dinner, over her roasted pheasant and his lobster, for him to bring up his proposal. By the time they had finished eating, there still had been no mention of the offer. Soon they returned to the dance floor where she stopped thinking constantly about his proposal until finally a dance ended and Matt held her hand as they returned to their table.

"Let's go out to my place and have something to drink and talk about my proposal. Is it too late for you?"

"No," she said, thankful she didn't have any early classes.

In minutes they were in his car and she turned in the seat to watch him drive. He glanced at her and back at the road. "What do you think so far? We're getting along."

"I agree. I'm still surprised you're interested. You've never given the slightest indication."

"I'm interested," he said. "And I've spent all day and most of tonight wanting to kiss you again," he said in a husky voice that stirred heat in her.

"We'll kiss, but I'm going home tonight. Alone. I'm not staying over," she said.

"I hadn't planned that you would," he answered easily. "I'm patient."

"I don't know where you live."

"I don't make much of an issue of it because I value my privacy. I won't give interviews at home or let the media photograph my house. That's another reason I like living here. I can maintain a certain degree of privacy without too big of a hassle. I can drive myself sometimes and I don't feel as if I have to have a bodyguard everywhere I go."

She hadn't even given a thought to limos or bodyguards.

He drove through tall iron gates that swung open when he punched a small handheld device. They wound up a drive to another iron gate that was opened by a gate-keeper. Matt spoke to the man before continuing on his way. She turned to look back as the gates closed. "How many people work for you here?"

He shook his head. "I'm not sure. I don't deal directly with my staff. I have someone who oversees the house-hold for me."

With each passing second, she became more amazed as she suspected Matt had intended she would be.

They rounded a bend and the forest vanished, re-placed by immaculate grounds with tall stately pines. "My word! You live in a castle," she said, awed by her first view of a palatial mansion with wings, balconies and a wide portico. A circular drive in front created a border for a well-lit garden of fall flowers. "I didn't know there was anything like this in the state. You guard your privacy well."

"That's right. I don't bring people home with me. There are other places to go and few women I see even live here in Cheyenne. It's easier that way."

"You may be making the most colossal mistake in asking me to be your wife," she said, letting out her breath. "This lifestyle is totally foreign to me. I knew you were wealthy. Now this makes it seem tangible."

"I'd think my offer to you would make it seem sub-stantial," he remarked dryly.

"No, your proposal still has a definite dreamlike quality."

"Your kiss last night didn't. It was very real," he said. "And so were the effects of it."

She smiled. "Maybe I can try again later," she flirted.

As Matt stopped in front, a man had come out to open the door for her. When she emerged from the car, the employee greeted Matt, who introduced her.

Matt took her arm and led her into the front hall. Beneath a sparkling crystal chandelier, water splashed in a fountain. Farther along the hall, two staircases spiraled to the second floor.

"I'll show you around later. First, let's relax in front of the fire where we can talk. What would you like to drink?"

"Hot chocolate sounds tasty."

"That's easy. Come with me," he said and they walked across the hall and into another spacious area with a fire roaring in the fireplace, floor-to-ceiling glass doors that opened onto an enclosed room that held a pool, fountains and flowers.

After placing a drink order on the intercom, Matt led her to a brown leather sofa. As he shed his jacket and tie and unfastened the top buttons of his shirt, she momentarily forgot her surroundings and was ensnared in watching Matt. When she was with him, longing was a steady smoldering fire that now fanned stronger. He looked casual, more approachable, his appeal intensifying.

"If you accept my proposal, this is where we'll live when we're in Cheyenne."

She looked around at one wall lined with shelves with an assortment of books, oil paintings, vases, bronze statues. The room was filled with leather furniture, a hickory floor, the huge stone fireplace, a plasma television. Had he brought her out here to intimidate her?

She faced him squarely. "I can't believe that I could ever be a part of this, even for a brief time."

"All you have to do is accept my offer."

"Did you bring me out here so I'll drop my conditions? It seems ridiculous to ask anything more of you when you're doing something that would enable me to live in this house."

He sat on the leather sofa. "Let's hear what you want."

She reminded herself that the worst he could do was refuse. In reality, the worst he could do would be to withdraw his proposal and tell her to get lost.

There was a light rap at the door and a maid appeared bearing a tray with cups of cocoa and a china pot with a lid, plus a plate of cookies.

"Thanks, Renita," he said. "Brianna, this is Renita, who has worked for me for several years now."

After Brianna greeted the woman, Renita turned to leave them alone, closing the door behind her.

"Now back to our subject," he said. "Your requests."

"I have a list," she said, getting out the paper and he smiled.

She held the folded paper in her hand. "Look, Matt, I'm the oldest child in my family. You are in your family, right?"

"Yes, I am."

"From the time I was about twelve years old, I pretty much had to run things at home for all five of my siblings. My mom has cleaned businesses all her life and she's worn out. When my dad was alive, he drank too much and he cheated on her all through the years. I could never be with someone who cheated."

"You won't have a problem with me on that score."

"Good, can we put it in a prenup agreement?"

"I don't think you need to write that one down," Matt said dryly. "I'll be faithful. By the way, once we marry, and I get into the investment group, I won't necessarily hold you to two years. If you want out sooner, a divorce wouldn't affect my role in that group. They have some members who are divorced."

"Seems a little inconsistent to me, but acceptable. Two years maximum, though, right?"

"Right. That will do."

"No problem there. Now the next thing. You're a very wealthy man. So much so that half a million up front and half a million later seems paltry by your standards."

A smile flitted over his face and disappeared, but amusement still danced in his eyes. "How much do you want, Brianna?"

His name rolling off her tongue gave her a tingle. And she felt a momentary panic for trying to wrest more money from him when a million dollars was a fantastic fortune she couldn't imagine earning on her own. Taking a quick breath, she looked him squarely in the eyes. "Two million up front and two million when we part. In addition, I want you to pay for a nanny for my baby as long as I need one. And put some money in trust for the baby's education."

"That's a lot of money. You're going to make some

more by being married to me, plus the car I promised and the clothes and you'll live in a manner you don't now have. I'll think about it. Anything else on that list?" he asked.

She held it closer to her as if to keep him from seeing it. "That covers it. I have a preference about waiting to sleep together until we've said vows," she said, her palms growing sweaty because he didn't appear to be willing to accept her terms about money. "I want to know each other better."

He looked amused. "I won't push that on you any-time you don't want to. Married or not," he answered easily.

She felt her face flush hotly and wished she could control her blushes. "You might consider that a strange request when I'm expecting. I'm pregnant because I partied and let go, celebrating exams being over. Oth-erwise, I've had one other guy in my past and that was in high school."

"I'll wait until you're ready."

The hot chocolate sat forgotten and she felt the tension increase. What she wanted and what he wanted were dif-ferent. There was no mistaking which one of them had the most power. If he took back his proposal, she wondered whether she would ever get over letting a million dollars slip through her fingers. Her heart was pounding so hard and fast, she thought he surely could hear it.

He gave her a long look and she almost blurted out to forget what she had requested.

"While we're into demands, I have one more that we

didn't settle last night when we talked. I want you to drop out of school."

"Now?" She was aghast and he asked the impossible.

"Now. In two years you can pick up where you left off."

The thought of losing momentum on her education set her back. It was the one thing she most wanted. Her degree and a nanny. She'd never had any substantial cash in her life, always living hand to mouth, but school was tangible and she had almost achieved part of her education goal.

"I want to finish this semester," she said. "It ends in December. That's not very long."

"Withdraw from college this week. I'd like to take you on a honeymoon. I'll want you to accompany me to Europe often. Your grades will suffer. You can pick school up again when we divorce and you'll be better off than trying to juggle classes *and* marriage *and* a baby. The baby will be two or more when you go back. Easier to handle."

The prospect hurt of giving up a goal she'd had since she was old enough to realize a degree would get her out of the poverty she'd been born into. Two years and she could go back. She would have a nanny, help and money, which would be infinitely easier.

"All right, I'll drop out," she said, feeling as if she were ripping part of herself away.

"Good. As for my part—I'll pay you *one* million up front and *one* million when we part and I'll provide nannies and that education trust fund," he said flatly.

"Thank you," she said, drawing a long breath as relief

filled her. She would still get two million dollars! Her heart was in her throat over wresting so much money out of him. She and her baby—and the rest of her family—were fixed for life, she was sure. There would be more than enough for all of them to go to college or trade school. Matt would provide a nanny for her baby. Financial worries fell away and she was giddy with excitement she couldn't contain.

Smiling at him, she scooted the distance that separated them to throw her arms around his neck. "I accept your proposal, Matt. I'll marry you!"

Four

The minute Brianna voiced her acceptance, her green eyes sparkled. Reaffirmation that he'd made a good choice swept Matt, sending his own enthusiasm soaring. She looked as if he had handed her the world on a silver tray—and well she should, he knew. It was also a look he never would have received from any other woman he'd considered wife material.

Wrapping his arms around her, Matt pulled her closer as they kissed. Soft, sweet-smelling and eager, she pressed against him, her tongue thrusting deep into his mouth as she poured herself into her kiss and set him ablaze. He wanted her more than ever. The thought that soon she would be totally his fanned the flames already raging in him.

He pulled her onto his lap to embrace her as he kissed her, slowly and thoroughly. Her soft moans, her hands running over his neck and shoulders, heightened his passion. Remembering that she wanted to wait for consummation rose dimly in the back of his mind, but her kisses sent another message.

He wound his fingers in her silky hair and longed to bury himself in her. Thought vanished and only the pounding of his heart and roaring of his pulse enveloped him. Holding her, he ran his hand down her back over the thin cotton of her shirt, lower over her cotton slacks to follow the curve of her bottom.

Continuing to kiss her, he cradled her against his shoulder. All of his senses were steeped in pleasure and she was turned in his arms to where he could caress her slender neck. His hand went lower, lightly across her breast. The instant he caressed a taut peak, she moaned and twisted her hips slightly, clutching his shoulders. Her softness and instant responses inflamed him.

He freed her top button to slide his hand beneath her shirt and bra to cup her breast while his thumb circled her nipple. She moaned again, a sound of enjoyment that heightened his own.

Raising her head, she grasped his wrist and pulled on his hand. "Wait, Matt," she whispered. Her plea halted him and he moved his hand, raking his fingers through her hair to comb it away from her face.

"This is too new," she said. "Slow down a little."

"Whatever you want," he said in a deep, husky tone that happened in passionate moments. His pulse still raced and he was hot with desire that he tried to cool. Her lips were red and swollen from his kisses, her face flushed. Her response to his kisses had been intense and he had to curb the impulse to pull her close again and try to kiss away her protests. If she would even protest further.

Scooting off his lap, she pulled her clothes in place and faced him on the sofa. "We have plans to make."

She retrieved her cup of cocoa and sipped it, holding the china cup with both hands.

"We're not in love, Brianna, so I think a small, quiet wedding would be more appropriate. Family and only close friends."

"That's all I would have anyway," she said.

"I'll pay for the wedding, so you'll have no worries there. Get the dress you want, but not formal. This won't be that big a deal. I'd like to marry as soon as possible. This is Friday. Can you marry a week from tomorrow?"

Her eyes widened and she seemed to be thinking about it. "I don't see why not," she replied.

"Excellent!" His pulse jumped again. He'd get into the investment group before the year was out, he guessed. "I'll clear my calendar and we'll take a week for a honeymoon." He pulled out his wallet and gave her a card. "Here, use this to buy clothes. If you can't find the wedding dress you want here, tell me and I'll fly you to San Francisco, Dallas or wherever you'd like to look. Monday we can open an account for you and transfer money."

"You don't waste time, do you?"

"Quit your job in the morning. You don't need it any

longer and they can get a new waitress. Not one as beautiful, though," he said, smiling at her.

She licked her lower lip and inhaled and he was sidetracked. He knew she was thinking about something besides her job. He slipped his hand behind her head to comb his fingers into her long hair. "We'll both benefit, Brianna. You'll see."

"I know it'll be a miracle for me," she said. Her ongoing wonder pleased him because it continued to confirm his choice. Nicole, or any other woman he'd known well, would never be awed. They'd be asking for more of his time and his attention, plus money.

"If you'd like, you can move in here right away," he said, hoping she'd accept.

Her eyes widened again and she looked around. "I can't picture living here."

"It's a home and comfortable and why not? After we marry you can move into my bedroom with me. There are twelve bedrooms in this house, so there's no lack of space," he remarked dryly.

"Maybe I'll move in Monday. It won't take long to pack my things."

"Do it tomorrow. Brianna, you're so early in your pregnancy that we can tell everyone the baby is mine."

She bit her lip and looked lost in thought. "I'd like that, but what happens if we stay together until my baby is a toddler? This baby will see you as Daddy by then. Besides, the baby will have my last name."

"I hadn't thought about that," he said, realizing this wasn't going to be as simple as he'd envisioned and he hadn't given enough attention to the prospect of a baby in his life. "Let me talk to my lawyer and accountant and I'll see what I can do."

She nodded as if satisfied by his answer.

"Maybe I can work it out where your baby has my name. If it reaches the media that it's not my baby, the news won't be earth-shattering anyway."

"Because by then you'll be in your investment group," she said and that cool tone she'd first used returned to her voice.

"That's right. This decision is up to you," he said. "I'd think you'd prefer it, too."

"I do, even though it may complicate our lives later."

"We can call our families right now so they can start making plans," Matt said.

"Are you going to leave the impression that we're in love, or are we going to tell our families this is a temporary marriage?" she asked.

"I'd just as soon say it was the real thing," he replied, having already given thought to what he wanted. "That way, when the press gets wind of this, there won't be a big scandal. Will that be a problem with your family?"

"No. I'm close with my mom and sisters and we'll talk. I'll need to bring them here a few days early so they can buy clothes for the wedding that I will pay for with your money," Brianna said.

"Unless you have a preference, we'll marry here at the house," Matt replied. "I'll get the minister. That way, I can keep this private."

"That's reasonable," she said. The more they talked,

the more he longed to pull her back into his arms and kiss her and forget their planning or waiting.

"Sunday morning I'll take you to church with me and you can meet the minister."

Matt pulled out a card and gave it to her. "Here's a card from the owner of a shop that has pretty dresses. It's a small shop and you see the address. Go look there tomorrow. She'll help you and you might find what you like for the wedding."

"I've seen their ads," Brianna said, taking the card from him, her fingers lightly brushing his. The slight contact added to his yearning to hold her in his arms again. "I couldn't ever afford a dress from this shop."

"Now you can, so go look and buy something if you see what you want. I'd like to have both of my older cousins as groomsmen and my two brothers as groomsmen, also."

"That will work for me because I'll have my sisters and my two closest friends," she said. "We've got our plans set for now, and I can feel the evening catching up with me. I should go, Matt."

"Certainly," he said, wondering if their plans would blow up in his face or work as smoothly as he hoped. Was he letting lust kill all his business judgment?

As if she guessed his thoughts, she gazed at him with a somber expression. "We're both jumping into this as if into a dark well."

"No, we're not," he said, his self-assurance kicking in full force. "I've given this thought. I know my proposal and my plans are new to you, but I've been living with them for a while. I think we'll both come out ahead."

"You're being driven by greed and love of money."

"And you're not?" he asked lightly, amused that she could see her own motives in a better light than his.

"This marriage has to make life better for my baby, me and even my family who'll benefit, too."

He hugged her. "Stop worrying and dwelling on the negative possibilities. We're into it now."

"Not absolutely until we say wedding vows," she said. Before he could reply, she spoke quickly. "I still want to go ahead. Don't misunderstand me. I'm glad you selected me."

He held open the door for her and walked to his car with her. "It's natural to have wedding jitters—and in this case, even more expected."

He closed the door and walked around the car, glad he'd planned to marry soon. If he could whisk her to a justice of the peace tomorrow, he'd do it, but he wanted this to appear to be the real thing for now and a big deal for both of them—which it was.

He drove her home, giving her a light kiss. "Think about the money, Brianna, and forget the rest. It's going to be worth your while and mine."

Matt's words rang in his ears early Monday morning when he went to his office. He'd only been there half an hour when his closest friend arrived and came in to see him.

As soon as Matt announced Brianna's acceptance of

his proposal, Zach glared at him. "You'll regret this more than anything you've ever done. You can pick stocks, but choosing a woman as you would a stock is going to be a disaster." Beneath a tangle of wavy blond hair, Zach's pale brown eyes filled with irritation.

Matt calmly faced him. "It's a done deal. We're engaged."

"You can get out of that and you know it. Get out fast. Marry Nicole. She's gorgeous, a socialite who moves in your world. She's wealthy in her own right, so she won't be after your money and she's not pregnant with another guy's baby. Another guy who may show up when he gets wind that the mother of his baby has landed a rich guy."

"The minute I get into that investment group, I don't care. I'm not worried about him, anyway. They went to an attorney and he signed away all rights to the baby. He's long gone from Wyoming."

"That can be broken in court and you know it."

"That's their fight. Not mine. But if it'll shut you up, we can have him found," Matt said, entering his schedule for the day into his BlackBerry.

"As your friend, I'm pleading with you not to marry this woman. She isn't in your social class. She only has waitress experience. She won't know how to deal with your lifestyle."

"Don't be ridiculous," Matt said with amusement. "You think I was born into this lifestyle?"

"You weren't as far removed from it as she is. She's from a tiny little town and plain."

"Her family is honest, aren't they? Never been in any criminal trouble?"

"No, but that's about all you can say for them. That's not the kind of person to lock yourself into a marriage contract with. She'll want more, I can promise you."

"She already has. She demanded more money."

"You've got to be kidding. And you agreed, didn't you?"

"Yep, I did. It's done, Zach. Now, get me a list of places she can put the money I'm about to give her. I'll meet with her later this morning and discuss what she wants to do."

Zach raked his fingers through his hair that sprang back in thick waves. He shook his head and threw his hands in the air. "I give up. I've said all I can say. I suppose you've told Nicole goodbye."

"She walked on me. She was unhappy that I wouldn't give her more of my time. I don't expect those demands from Brianna. I promise you, she's not going to bore me," Matt replied, smiling at his friend. "Think you can have a list in an hour?"

"Sure. I'll get someone working on it right away and I'll go over it… I wish I could dissuade you."

"I'm grown, Zach. I know what I want. She's perfect."

"I'll try to avoid saying 'I told you so' later," Zach grumbled and left the room.

Matt gazed at the empty doorway and wondered if Zach would prove to be right. He couldn't imagine being bored by Brianna. At the moment, he couldn't wait to be with her. He picked up the phone to call his chief attorney.

* * *

Twenty-four hours later, seated in a quiet, high-priced restaurant, Matt glanced at his watch impatiently. After Matt's lunch appointment with Zach, Brianna was going to meet him at the restaurant at one. If Zach didn't show soon, Matt realized he was going to run late for Brianna. Zach was already ten minutes behind. Zach had asked for the lunch appointment away from the office and Matt couldn't imagine the reason. It was uncharacteristic of Zach, who was as much of a workaholic as Matt.

"Matt?"

He heard the familiar voice and glanced around to see Nicole slide into the seat facing him. She looked as gorgeous as ever in a white designer suit with bright red accessories that complemented her pale blond hair. She smiled at him. "Don't get angry at Zach. I asked him to do this because I want to talk to you."

Matt kept his temper in check over Zach's high-handed interference, wondering how much of the blame Nicole shared.

A waiter appeared with glasses of water, took their order and left.

"I ought to walk out now," Matt said easily.

"Please don't. I want to talk to you. I really am responsible for this. I heard from someone that you're thinking about getting engaged to that waitress."

"Nicole, we're through."

Nicole shuddered and gulped. "I suppose I deserve this for getting in such a huff the last time we were together, but I know you're not in love. I know the only thing keeping you out of that investment group was your bachelor status."

"Not any longer."

"Matt, don't do this. You can break the engagement. We had a wonderful relationship for a while and we can have it again," she said, beginning to sound desperate. He wished Zach hadn't set him up for this encounter.

He shook his head. "You should have just phoned me, Nicole, and saved yourself the trouble. I intend to marry her. It's over between us. You made that abundantly clear."

"Matt!" she cried, interrupting him. "I'm sorry if I demanded too much of your time. Stop and think how wonderful we were together. She means nothing to you. You barely know her."

"This is my decision," he answered patiently, wishing lunch were over and he could escape. He looked at her flawless skin and wide eyes. She was a stunning woman and once upon a time, she'd set his heart pounding, but she didn't mean anything now, nor did he find her desirable. He realized it was finished—if he'd ever truly cared for her at all. Idly, he wondered how long it would be until he would feel that way regarding Brianna.

"Give us another chance," Nicole urged, leaning across the table to caress his hand lightly while she talked. "It was incredible between us—you know it was."

"Nicole, this is an absolutely useless conversation." Matt stopped talking as the waiter approached with a tray of food. He placed a salad in front of Nicole and a sandwich in front of Matt.

She smiled at him and raised her water glass in a toast. "Then here's to the happy bridegroom. May your future be filled with joy."

"I'll drink to that one," he said, touching her glass with his and sipping the icy water.

As they ate, Nicole was her most charming, switching totally from the subject of Brianna, yet Matt knew she was deliberately trying to entertain and charm him as a reminder of how good things could be between them. He struggled to pay attention to her conversation and tried to avoid being obvious when he glanced occasionally at his watch. He had to get rid of Nicole before Brianna appeared.

To his consternation, Nicole selected a dessert. Matt asked the waiter for the check and then as soon as they were alone, Matt faced Nicole. "I'm sorry, I have an appointment. I'll get the lunch and you can take your time. I have to leave."

She smiled at him. "That's all right, Matt. I still wish you'd think about what I've said to you. It's not too late to get out of this engagement. You'll be incredibly bored with her."

"That's for me to worry about," he replied easily.

Their waiter returned and Matt settled up.

As the waiter turned away, Matt glanced across the dining room and saw Brianna approaching the table. As he started to stand, she looked from him to Nicole and then back at him and he could see her surprise. She stopped and then turned, rushing away from him.

"Nicole, I have to go," Matt said.

"*She's* your appointment?" Nicole protested, stepping to block his path as she grasped his wrist.

"Move out of my way, Nicole," he said quietly.

"Don't leave. Stay here, Matt. Give us another chance together because what we had was great."

"Goodbye, Nicole," he said.

"Matt—"

In spite of her calling his name, he rushed through the restaurant and outside, to watch Brianna climb into her car. He ran across the lot in the warm sunshine. When she backed out of the parking place and turned, he stepped in front of her car to prevent her from leaving. She honked as he stood with his hands on the hood of the car. Certain she wouldn't hurt him, he had no intention of letting her drive away until he talked to her.

In seconds, she opened her window and thrust her head out. "Matt, move out of my way."

"No. I want you to promise to listen to me."

She glared at him a moment and then cut the motor. He knew she could start up and race away and he wouldn't be able to stop her, but he wasn't going to get anywhere by standing in front of her car. He walked around to climb in on the driver's side. "Move over," he ordered.

With another glare at him, she did as he asked, climbing over the gear shift to sit on the passenger side. He slid behind the wheel, started the car and pulled back into a parking place, where he cut the motor once again and turned to face her.

"That wasn't what you're thinking. You pay attention

to my explanation," he said, determined to get her to listen to the truth. He had no intention of allowing an unwanted encounter with Nicole to harm his future.

Five

Brianna locked her fingers together and nodded. She had feared all along that Matt wouldn't be faithful to her, but she hadn't expected to find him with someone else before they were married.

"I didn't plan that lunch with Nicole," he said firmly, gazing into her eyes. "I thought I was having lunch with Zach, a guy who works for me."

Brianna didn't believe him and waited in silence.

"Nicole said she asked Zach to get me to lunch so she could talk to me. I was already there when she appeared and we went ahead and ate lunch. That's all it was."

"I find that difficult to believe. You forget I've waited on your table when you're together."

"Brianna, do you think I'd make a lunch date with

another woman when I knew I was meeting you at the same restaurant? I've got more sense than that if I'd intended to do any such thing."

She gazed at him, realizing that was probably true. As she began to believe him, her hurt eased. She had been shocked and furious to discover him with Nicole, but she knew what he'd said was logical. Now she really looked at him without a haze of fury. Black curls tumbled on his forehead and his jacket was unbuttoned, revealing a crisp white shirt. His navy tie was slightly askew. Otherwise, he appeared as composed as ever.

"All right, Matt. I believe you," she said. "It shocked me to see you together today. I know she's been a big part of your life."

"That's past. I promise you, she's out of my life now and she won't be back in it."

"But she wants in it, doesn't she?" Brianna asked, hoping she was wrong. Disappointment surged when he nodded.

"Yes, she does. I told her, and I promise *you*, it's all over with her. You and I have a deal. I feel nothing when I'm with her."

Brianna studied him, wondering if he would be saying the same words about her someday. It was decided that their marriage would be over in a maximum of two years. In the future would she be referred to as casually as he dismissed Nicole now?

He leaned forward to tilt her chin up so she looked into his eyes. "You're the woman in my world. By this time next week you'll be my wife. I don't want any other woman. Okay?"

"Okay," she said, her gaze lowering to his mouth. He was only inches away now and her irritation had been replaced by desire. "I don't intend to share you," she said.

"You won't have to," she dimly heard him say, but her pounding heart was dulling his words and she raised her mouth to his as she slipped her arm around his neck. His mouth came down on hers and her lips opened beneath his. His kiss was hot, demanding, confirming that she was his woman in a way words never could.

Worries and concerns about other women in his life ceased to exist. Now all she wanted were Matt's kisses. They were leaning over the gear shift of her car and she realized they were still in the parking lot of the restaurant, so she pushed lightly on Matt's chest.

"We're in public," she whispered. "And this is less than the perfect place to kiss," she added, scooting away from him.

"We have appointments this afternoon, but I would like to cancel all of them and take you home with me."

"You can't," she said, smiling at him. "Not if you want to stay on schedule for a wedding this weekend."

"There's something else, Brianna. We will honeymoon in Rome because there's a charity ball I want to attend. I'd already agreed to appear and I'd still like to go because members of the investment group will be there and I'll have a chance to chat with them and introduce you as my wife. I'm telling you so you can buy a dress for the occasion. Get something elegant and don't worry about expense."

"Rome…?"

Intimidated by the thought of participating in a charity gala with him and meeting his investment acquaintances, her smile vanished. She knew she would be out of her element.

"Matt," she said hesitantly, and his eyes narrowed. "Are you certain you want me to accompany you to something like that immediately after we get married? I haven't ever attended a charity ball."

"You'll dazzle them," he said. "And I'm very sure about taking you. I want you there with me. If you need someone to coach you, I can get someone."

"Not at all," she answered, trying to cover her uncertainties and fears. As soon as possible, she knew she should start getting ready for the ball and practicing her Italian.

She reflected that he would also be working in Italy. As carefully as he'd charted his marriage to help him get into his investment group, so his honeymoon would give him a chance to promote his marriage and show her to the European investors. His constant eye on his goal jarred her until she reminded herself that she had a contract with him. There was no love in this union, so why wouldn't the honeymoon be a business trip?

Brianna glanced at her watch. "We're going to be late for our meeting at the bank today. After that, I see the wedding planner."

"Given the amount I put into accounts for you yesterday, the banker won't mind if we're a few minutes late," Matt said, his heated expression conveying his fervor. "I'll drive and we'll come back to get my car."

Gazing out the car window, she thought about having to stop by the university again today. Even though she'd dropped out of her classes, she wanted to figure some way by next semester to continue her education because Matt would be often occupied with his work. She suspected after their honeymoon, she would have huge chunks of time when she could study. He might want her out of his life as soon as he was accepted into his investment group. She intended to get all she could out of this brief union.

Wednesday, she stopped at Matt's office.

She stepped into the lobby that had enormous planters with tall, exotic greenery, palms, banana trees, tropical plants that were at least eight feet tall. A fountain splashed in the center of the lobby.

First she had to deal with security, but her name was on a list and she was ushered toward the elevators.

As she walked away from the security desk, she heard the low voice of the employee telling someone that she was headed toward the top floor and Matt's office.

When she stepped out into a thickly carpeted hallway, light spilled through the glass walls. More potted plants and leather benches lined the hallway. A stocky blond man stepped out of an office and approached her.

"Miss Costin?" he asked, his gaze raking over her as he frowned. "I'm Zach Gentner. Matt has been momentarily detained in a meeting. If you'll come with me, I'll show you into his office. You can wait there."

"Thank you," she said, smiling and relaxing slightly beneath his friendly smile.

They walked through a large reception area where she met a receptionist and then through a smaller office where she met Matt's private secretary.

She followed Zach into a spacious office with light spilling through two glass walls. The carpet was plush, the dark walnut paneling a complementary backdrop to the brown leather furniture with oil paintings of Wyoming landscapes on the walls and the two tall bronze statues of a stalking mountain lion and galloping horses on tables.

"Congratulations on your engagement, Miss Costin," Zach said.

"Thank you," she said, feeling uncomfortable in spite of his congratulations.

"Your family should be extremely proud of you—you have money now for your baby, a comfortable future and endless opportunities. I hope you can always remember the sacrifices Matt has made to take a total stranger as his wife, in a less than satisfying business arrangement that locks him into a loveless marriage."

His sarcastic words hit her with the pain of a knife thrust. Her smile vanished and she chilled. "It was his choice," she replied stiffly.

"I know it was. I heard you made even greater demands, which he caved to. I hope you don't ruin his life. Of course, if he doesn't get in that group, he'll dump you so fast your head will spin. How long this fake marriage will last anyway, is anybody's guess. Until he tires of your body or you are quite large with child."

She clamped her hands together and bit her lip, trying to keep calm and think before she replied to his hurtful words. "You obviously don't approve of me," she said, forcing her voice to stay low and controlled, determined she wouldn't let him goad her into losing her temper.

"Not at all," he said, "but it isn't my choice. While I've told him what I think, he's stubborn. I hate to see him hurt or watch you ruin his life. You're pregnant with some other guy's baby from a one-night stand, not the best recommendation for marriage. Only you know if that guy is really the father or if it's someone else."

"He's the father," she said quietly, livid with fury that she was determined to keep in check. "Are you overstepping your bounds as an employee, Mr. Gentner? Aren't you afraid Matt will be furious to learn about this conversation?"

"Not at all," he answered coldly. "He'll know I did it for his own good. We go back a long way. Almost as far back as those cousins of his whom I almost called to see if either of them could talk sense into him. That confounded bet is the reason for this ridiculous proposal you have.

"Of course, they're so competitive, they'll see this marriage as a way of eliminating Matt from the running. They'll know he'll get out of this marriage eventually. I hope it doesn't cost him too much money. I know it won't cost emotionally because he doesn't have one shred of love for you. I'm sure that's no secret. Matt is up-front about business deals he makes and that's all this sham marriage is."

"I don't want to listen to this," she said, heading toward the door. "You tell—"

Matt strode into the room. "Brianna, I'm sorry I'm late." He broke off his words as his eyes narrowed. Looking back and forth between Zach and her, he focused on her. "Is something wrong?"

"Maybe for him—"

Zach spoke in a slightly louder tone, drowning her out. "I was congratulating your fiancée on her engagement and upcoming union. I'll leave you two alone," Zach said, leaving the room in haste.

Matt watched him go and then turned to study Brianna. He walked to her to place his hands on her shoulders and continue to gaze at her with a probing stare. "What's happened? What did he say to you?"

"He hopes I don't ruin your life," she answered quietly. "I simply assume you're doing what you want to do and you've given your proposal thought."

"Damn!" Matt said softly. "Forget Zach. Damn straight I've given it thought and I'm doing exactly what I want. Don't think about him or what he's said. I'll talk to him about it later."

"Don't get into a fight over it. I'll forget what he said," she stated, knowing in reality she would never forget.

As she looked up at Matt, it was easy to forget the past few minutes and Zach's hurtful words because Matt gazed at her with such desire in his expression that Zach no longer mattered.

"Brianna, there's something else. I've talked to my lawyer and thought over what I want to do. I'll adopt your baby so the child will have my name, the same as if it were my own."

She gasped with surprise. "You'd do that?"

"It seems the best way. Sooner or later, we'll divorce, but the baby will have my name and I can pay child support."

"Matt!" The enormity of how badly he wanted this marriage made her weak in the knees. "You'd do all that to get more money?"

"I'm doing a lot of it to get you," he said in a husky voice, drawing her closer to him.

She couldn't believe that he really meant what he said. They weren't in love, but whatever his reason, she was going to accept before he had time to reconsider. There was no way his adopting her baby would be bad. "Matt, I hope you really know what you're doing," she said. "It's acceptable to me."

"I thought it would be. I don't see how else we can deal with your baby."

Once again, she wished love was in the mix. Matt's words should have been thrilling, but his offer sounded too businesslike to give her a deep joy. Even so, she was glad for her baby's sake, and his offer gave her another degree of security.

"Now don't worry about Zach or your baby or our future," Matt said.

She wound her arms around Matt's neck. "This is what's important. If you're content, then I'm satisfied."

When he picked her up, she tightened her arms around his neck as he gave her a long kiss that shut out the world.

* * *

Before the rehearsal dinner Friday night, she took deep gulps of air and tried to relax as she waited in her suite for her family to gather before leaving for Matt's. His family was staying with him. She had moved to the hotel where she had booked suites for her family and herself. Members of both families and friends in his wedding party and their spouses planned to gather at Matt's home for hors d'oeuvres and to get acquainted. Then after the wedding rehearsal, they'd leave for an extravagant restaurant.

She was incredibly nervous over Matt meeting her family for the first time. Her family had never been far from Blakely, where they'd grown up. She was the first and only to finish high school, the first to attend college and they knew little about etiquette or table manners. She had spent the past three days getting them new clothes and haircuts, which Brianna could easily afford now. At each meal she had coached them on table manners, with an etiquette book open in front of her for quick reference.

Her family was to meet in the sitting room of Brianna's spacious suite and her mother was the first to arrive.

Adele Costin had been transformed and Brianna gazed at her mother with joy. "Mom, you look great!"

"I have you to thank for it," she replied, smiling at her daughter. "Look, my first manicure. I can't recognize my own hands or my hair or my image in the mirror, for that matter," she said, laughing and holding out her hands. Her mother had spent a lifetime cleaning and Brianna could remember her red, chapped hands.

Now they looked lovely with a pale pink polish on her well-shaped nails.

Her mother's tailored navy suit was attractive and flattering. Her black, slightly graying hair was cut short and combed straight to highlight the soft contours of her face.

"You look wonderful, Mom," Brianna said again and kissed her mother's cheek.

"I hope you are pleased, Brianna, although at the moment, I don't see how you could possibly keep from being joyous. But money isn't everything."

"Mom, I'm happy," Brianna said. "I'm doing what I want to do. We're alone for a minute now, and there's something I want to tell you, but it's not for the rest of the family yet."

"What's that?" Adele asked.

"I'm expecting a baby."

"Oh, Brianna! A baby!" her mother exclaimed, smiling at her and hugging her briefly. Stepping away, she frowned and then leaned closer to study Brianna intently. "Are you happy about the baby?"

"Oh, yes! Of course. And now I'll be taken care of so well and I can help the whole family."

"The whole family isn't what you need to be concerned about. I want you to be really pleased," Adele said quietly.

"I am," Brianna replied, smiling at her mother. "I really am, Mom. I wouldn't be getting married if I didn't want to."

Her mother studied her as she nodded her head. "I hope so, and I want you to tell me if you need me."

"I will, I promise," Brianna said. "Now you'll be a grandmother again."

Appearing to relax, her mother had a faint smile, and Brianna was relieved that the worried look had vanished, at least for now. "A grandmother!" Adele said. "Ah, Brianna, that fills me with more hope for the future and gives me another purpose in life."

Brianna laughed. "You have plenty of purposes in life because you already have grandchildren."

"Each one is precious. Is Matt happy about the baby?"

"Yes, he's okay with everything," she answered carefully, trying to stick as close to the truth as she could. "Now don't start looking worried," Brianna said. "I'd rather not tell the rest of the family until after we've had the wedding. I'll tell them soon afterward, but I wanted you to know."

"That's fine. I can keep the secret, and you don't look as if you're pregnant. How far along are you?"

"Not far at all. The baby is due next summer—late June. We'll announce it soon."

"I understand. I want to meet this man who'll be my son-in-law."

"I think you'll like him," Brianna said, knowing Matt would probably charm her mother and all the rest of her family. "I'm nervous about tonight and meeting his family," Brianna admitted.

"You look beautiful, and he's lucky to get you as his bride."

Brianna smiled and brushed a kiss on her mother's cheek. "I love you, Mom."

"Your sisters are probably going to guess anyway, but your brothers never will. They won't say anything to me about it, though, nor will I to them."

"That's fine," Brianna said, feeling better now that she'd shared her news with her mother and wishing she could tell her everything about this marriage that was really a loveless union.

A knock at the door interrupted them, and Brianna's sister Melody entered with her children in tow.

Brianna smiled broadly, holding out her arms to hug the children. "Everyone looks so great!" Melody's hair had been cut as well, hanging straight with blond streaks, and her plain black dress was short enough to show off her long, shapely legs.

"So do you, Brianna," Melody replied. "Thanks for the dresses, the hotel, the haircuts. Everything is a dream."

Dressed and subdued, Phillip, who was four, and three-year-old Amanda, as well as the other children, would have two nannies to watch them after the rehearsal while the rest of the family went out to dinner.

"You think I look good," Melody said. "Wait until you see the transformation of the guys. You won't know them."

"I hope so," Brianna teased, "since they're usually working on cars in overalls covered in grease."

When her brothers and brothers-in-law entered, she saw what her sister had been talking about. Shaved, shorn and attired in conservative suits with white dress shirts and navy ties, the men had been transformed.

"Mercy! You guys do clean up well."

"So does everyone," said her youngest brother, Josh,

whose black hair was spiked in the front and combed down smoothly otherwise.

"I'm so proud of my family," she said, smiling at them. "And I want all of you to have a good time. Matt is a wonderful guy. Now, if everyone is ready, let's go."

"I can't wait to see this place," Melody said. "I've threatened the kids to behave and not touch anything."

"She's not kidding," Melody's husband, Luke, said. "She threatened me, too."

Laughter followed his announcement and more joking until Brianna raised her voice.

"Matt has limos waiting to take us to his house. Shall we go?"

As they rode through Cheyenne in the limousines provided by Matt, her nervousness returned. Once again, she experienced the same trepidation that she'd felt upon arriving in Cheyenne and again, on her first visit to the university campus. She was too aware of the limitations of her early years, her lack of cosmopolitan experiences or experience with a polite, more sophisticated segment of society. Momentarily, she envied Matt his background and his colossal self-assurance. Yet if they'd been born into the reverse circumstances, so Matt had come out of the backwoods, she couldn't imagine that he wouldn't carry off the transition to an urbanite with the same confidence and aplomb he exhibited daily now.

Her stomach churned with something worse than butterflies. Her palms were damp and she wondered if she could get herself and her family through this evening intact, or if Matt would rescind his proposal.

A uniformed man opened the door, but the minute she stepped inside, Matt was there to greet her. As soon as she saw him, her worries evaporated. Her heartbeat raced for a different reason and eagerness replaced worry.

"Am I glad to see you," he said softly, walking up to her to smile at her. "You are breathtaking and I wish we were alone for the night."

"Matt, I'll confess, I'm so nervous about tonight. You know this entire week is new to my family."

"Relax, Brianna, my family won't bite. We're here to have a good time and get ready for a wedding. Let me make an announcement to everyone and then we can do the introductions."

"Sure, whatever you want to do," she said, thankful to turn the moment over to him.

"Folks," Matt said in a deep, authoritative voice. To her surprise, he got everyone's attention and the room became silent.

"I'm Matt Rome and welcome to Cheyenne and to our rehearsal dinner. I want to thank you for coming to share this time with Brianna and with me. Now, why don't we go around the room and say our names and what relation we are. Brianna, we'll start with you."

When each of Matt's relatives spoke, she paid close attention, noticing Jared Dalton and Chase Bennett, the cousins she'd heard so much about. As her family introduced themselves, she watched each one, assessing her handiwork. Again, she focused on Danielle, whose brown hair was twisted and pinned at the back of her head. Danielle's three-year-old, Hunter, and two-year-old Emma, were as subdued as their cousins.

Finally the last person spoke, and then everyone's attention returned to Matt.

"Thanks again for coming and let's all enjoy the party! Help yourselves to drinks and hors d'oeuvres. In about an hour we'll have the rehearsal. Dinner will follow at a restaurant," Matt announced and then turned to her and people began to talk.

"Brianna, meet Megan and Jared Dalton and Laurel and Chase Bennett."

"Ah, the famous cousins," she said after greeting each in turn. Jared and Chase grinned.

"And our infamous bet," Chase added. "I think some family members are taking bets on who'll win," he said. As the men began to talk and joke about their bet, Megan took Brianna's arm. "You come with us. We've heard enough about that bet to last a lifetime," she said, pulling Brianna aside while Laurel nodded and joined them. "I suspect Megan and I wouldn't be married if it hadn't been for that bet," Laurel added dryly. "Whatever happens, the winner treats the rest to a weekend getaway, so we'll all have a wonderful weekend together."

"Those three are so competitive, yet they are truly close," Laurel said, glancing at her husband, who was nearby. The love in her gaze gave Brianna a pang, because she didn't feel that way with Matt, nor did he love her. This marriage simply secured her future. A future alone with her baby.

"This is exciting," Megan said, "and a big surprise to us. Jared didn't expect Matt to get married ever."

"Nor did Chase," Laurel added with a smile. "But then not too long ago, neither Jared nor Chase expected to marry. Life is filled with surprises."

Brianna listened as the two women talked and it was obvious that they were becoming friends although they seldom saw each other. She was glad to be included in their friendship, even though she knew it would be short-lived.

Soon she excused herself and began to circulate, going to talk to Faith, her friend who would be a bridesmaid.

"I'm so happy for you," Faith said, her light brown eyes sparkling. "This house is a dream home! I can't believe this is your house now—except I know it is."

Brianna laughed at Faith's exuberance, a relief after the tension she'd felt around her family who didn't really know the whole story.

"This is it," she said, realizing she was losing her awe about it since she'd moved in with Matt. "My first time here, I felt overwhelmed—as you should remember."

"This is the best thing that could possibly happen."

"I don't know so much about the best, but it will be good."

"Good. Stop being so pessimistic and such a worrier. He'll fall in love with you. And how could you possibly keep from falling in love with him? He's charming."

"He is that," Brianna agreed. "I'm glad you're here. I hope you're always close by. And I hope we always stay friends."

"I'm going to love having a friend like you. Have me over for a swim sometime. I've seen that pool. Mercy!"

Brianna laughed. "Wait until the honeymoon is over, and I'll call you and we can swim. Weather won't matter. Thanks for being in my wedding."

"I wouldn't miss this for the world. Thanks for inviting Cal to this, too. He likes your brothers."

"I'm glad. I hope Matt does. And vice versa, but then I expect all my family to like him. Let's get together soon. I've missed seeing you."

"Just call."

"I better go talk to Matt's family because I haven't yet."

"Get going. I'll see you later," Faith said, smiling at Brianna.

Moving through the guests and relatives, Brianna stopped to meet and talk to Matt's mother. Penny Rome put her arms around Brianna to hug her lightly. "Welcome to the family!" she said warmly. "We're so happy to see Matt marry. His dad and I'd given up on him."

"Thank you," Brianna said, smiling at Matt's tall, slender mother.

"You must be good for him—he seems more relaxed now. He's too much like his dad—constantly working whether it's necessary or not. Both of them are driven, as I guess you know about Matt by now. This marriage is good for him and we're thrilled."

"I'm glad," Brianna answered. Guilt assaulted her for the fake marriage, but she pushed it aside in her mind. If it hadn't been her, it would have been another woman.

She met and talked with his father—seeing instantly that was where Matt got his handsome looks as they both had the same coloring and features. "Welcome to our family. Mom and I are happy to see Matt settle and marry. He needs that in his life."

"Thank you," she replied politely.

"I hope you'll bring him to see us. We don't see much of him, but I understand that better than his mother does."

"We'll do that, Mr. Rome," she said.

"Brianna, you're in our family now. Call me Travis, or call me Dad if you want."

"Yes, sir. Thank you." She chatted a few minutes longer with him and then they were joined by one of Matt's sisters and Travis Rome moved away. His relatives seemed to accept her into their family and they were all friendly enough that her nervousness ebbed.

She discovered her own relatives were also enjoying themselves and at ease with Matt's side of the family. To her delight, she realized that the men in both families had a down-to-earth common thread of being cowboys, which cut across all levels of society.

Time passed quickly until they boarded limousines and were driven to dinner at an elegant restaurant. As she sat in the restaurant, she gazed at the array of silver cutlery and the crystal and was thankful she had bought an etiquette book and had been studying and coaching her family. Reaching for a shrimp fork, she felt more relaxed and assured than she would have a week earlier.

The one flaw in a perfect evening was Zach Gentner. He shook hands with her, greeting her with a coldness that mirrored her own. She hadn't given any thought to Zach being present, but if he was as close to Matt as he'd said, then he would be included in the wedding party.

During the evening, there was never a moment alone with Matt and she returned to the hotel with her family, going to her suite where she was finally alone. Long into the night she sat up. The next morning would be her wedding, and she was already too far in now to back out of the agreement even if she had wanted to. To her relief, her family had made it through the evening without too many obvious blunders. Hopefully, Matt's money would help give them the opportunities they needed to better their lives.

Tomorrow night the wedding would be over and she would legally be Mrs. Matt Rome. Merely thinking about it gave her a flutter of anticipation.

Finally the moment arrived to step into the large room where they were to be married. Both families and a few close friends were standing as an organist played and Brianna walked in with her arm linked with her youngest brother's. She met Matt's gaze. In a navy suit and tie, he looked handsome, confident and pleased. She felt assured about her appearance—having checked a dozen times before leaving the room where she dressed. Even though her knee-length white silk suit was plain, she liked its simple lines. A diamond and sapphire necklace wedding gift from Matt sparkled around her throat and a gorgeous diamond engagement ring sparkled on her finger. Tiny white rosebuds bedecked her pinned-up black hair.

Her brother placed her hand in Matt's and then she turned to gaze into his eyes as she said vows that she knew would be broken eventually. How hollow the words rang in her ears! For an instant guilt assailed her over the farce they were perpetrating, but then she remembered what each one was gaining. If it hadn't been her, it would have been another woman. She reminded herself again of the things she intended to do to care for her mother, the things that she would be able to do for herself.

After a brief kiss from Matt, they walked out of the room together as newlyweds.

The party commenced in one of his large reception rooms. Outside, flakes of snow swirled while fires blazed in each big fireplace and a band serenaded them.

When Matt drew her into his arms for the first dance, he smiled at her. "For a small wedding, we gathered quite a crowd. We each have sizable families."

"I can't imagine what a large wedding would have been like. This one is huge to me," she said, barely aware of her conversation because most of her attention was on the handsome man dancing with her. Her pulse raced and she was eager to be alone with him. She was conscious of their legs brushing, of her hand enclosed in his warm grasp. As she gazed up into his eyes, she could see the change from the polite smile he had been giving friends and family all day. Desire blazed in the depths of his crystal-blue eyes.

"This is great, Brianna," he said.

"Yes, it is. I'm still overwhelmed and overjoyed. Matt, you've been so good to my family. You were nice and patient with them."

"They're friendly people," he answered.

"Unless they get snowed in, they're all leaving to-morrow morning to drive home. This snow is supposed to stop soon, so it shouldn't amount to much."

"Have you told any of them about our arrangement?" he asked and she shook her head.

"No one. They've heard of you and now they've seen your house and had this weekend, but they don't know the extent of the wealth. They think I'm fortunate, but they have their lives and they'll return to their routines tomorrow. This weekend will be a memory."

"I thought maybe they'd want a bit more after this weekend."

"No. I don't think they've guessed quite what I can do."

"My family is staying here and we can leave before the party breaks up. Why don't we in an hour?" he suggested, and her heart missed a beat. They were leaving here and tonight this marriage would be consummated. She tingled with anticipation.

"Whenever you say," she whispered. "We still need to cut the—"

"I'll come get you at an opportune time," he broke in. He moved on in the crowd and after cutting the cake, for the next hour, she chatted and smiled constantly and hoped she didn't say anything that was nonsense because her attention was half on the handsome man she had married. She had never liked the Cinderella fairy tale because it seemed the antithesis of real life. Prince Charming didn't come along and transform the life of his love, someone poor and uneducated. She didn't expect that to happen, couldn't even imagine it happened. Yet today, the moment she became Mrs. Matthew Rome, it had occurred. She now had money, a hefty savings, investments and a large bank account plus more cash in her purse at one time than she'd ever had in her life.

She watched Matt with a circle of friends, women gazing up at him adoringly, men laughing and joking with him. A beautiful brunette stood close to him with her hand on his arm while she told him something and the group laughed. There was no reason for any jealousy. Married or single, Matt would always have other women after him, but she expected him to keep his promise to remain faithful as long as they were married.

As she watched, Matt took a cell phone out of his pocket and walked away from the crowd to head toward the hall. A couple came up to talk and then a friend appeared who asked her to dance and she lost Matt in the crowd.

Matt listened to one of his analysts discuss an acquisition while he threaded his way through the guests and into the hallway. Replacing the phone in his pocket, Matt heard a familiar voice and turned to face his cousin Chase.

"I thought you might like a drink," Chase said, handing Matt a glass of wine.

"Thanks. One glass of champagne is about all I can bear."

"You have a beautiful bride."

"Thanks, I think so. So do you."

"Thank you. The difference is, I'm in love with mine," Chase said quietly.

Matt gazed into his cousin's green eyes that were steady and filled with what looked like pity. "How'd you know?"

"When you know someone as well as you and I and Jared know each other, it shows," Chase said, flicking his head slightly so stray locks of his straight brown hair would go back into place above his forehead.

"My folks have been fooled."

"They probably don't want to know the truth. I think I can guess why you did it. Jared told me he asked Megan for a marriage of convenience, but she wouldn't have any part of it, and then later they fell in love all over again."

"So Jared knows, too," Matt said, wondering how many others in his family realized the truth.

"Yep, and I didn't tell him. We both came to the same conclusion before we ever said anything to each other. In some ways maybe this bet wasn't such a great idea. If our wager thrust you into a loveless marriage—"

"Whoa," Matt interrupted. "I'm delighted and she's thrilled. She's getting two mil for this marriage and I'm having a dream affair that I would have pursued anyway, wedding or not. We're very content."

"You may be pleased, but you're not in love. There's a vast difference. Even so, it's good to hear that this isn't quite the business arrangement Jared and I assumed it was."

"It isn't remotely a purely business arrangement. I think she's fantastic."

"She's a beauty and very charming. Maybe before too long you both will be in love. Here's hoping you are."

Matt smiled. "Don't count on that one."

"I'm glad she's getting money out of the deal, and I hope that she thinks it's worth it to be hitched to you."

"If I do say so myself, I think the lady looks happy."

"That she does. And may you both be fulfilled in your bargain." Chase held out his drink. They touched glasses and sipped their wine.

"Where'd you find her? What debutante list? She looks younger."

"She's twenty-three. She's been going to college, she's from a tiny backwoods town, she's never been out of Wyoming and she's never flown in a plane."

Chase laughed. "So both of you are in for big changes."

"One of us is."

Chase chuckled. "You may be caught in a bramble bush of your own making. She told me she wants to get a law degree."

"I have no doubt that she will. Now she can easily afford to enroll."

"No problem there. She could have a zilch IQ and with her looks and as your wife, it wouldn't matter." Chase's mouth curled in a crooked grin. "Unless—"

"Unless what?" Matt narrowed his eyes, knowing he shouldn't even ask.

"Unless she's really smart and gives you a run for your money." Chase chuckled. "That would be fun. At least for Jared and me to watch, although you'll never let us know if you come out holding the short end of the stick. Or if you fall in love and she dumps you. 'Course that one, we might know."

"Right. Quit wringing your hands with glee—it won't happen. And I intend to win our bet."

Chase had a wide grin this time. "Sure, coz. We all aim to do that. And one of us will. We each have our own idea about who it will be."

"Speaking of my wife, I want to find her. Where's Laurel?"

"Dancing with an old friend the last I saw. I wish you luck, coz," Chase said with a grin as the two men went in search of their wives.

Brianna listened to someone who was speaking in the cluster of people around her, yet her mind was on Matt.

Soon now they could escape the party, get away to themselves. Anticipation continued to grow. A dark cloud loomed on her horizon—this marriage was as loveless as it was temporary.

She knew the one thing she had to constantly remember was Matt's true nature and love of money.

And then she caught his gaze and her pulse jumped. Across the large room, too far apart to communicate, someone who had been a stranger to her only a short time ago, now could exchange a glance with her and send her pulse into overdrive.

Still watching, she knew when he excused himself and began to move through the crowd toward her. Soon her life would really begin as Mrs. Matt Rome.

Six

That night, Matt carried her over the threshold of his Manhattan penthouse overlooking Central Park, a mere private jet flight away. Setting her on her feet, he wrapped his arms around her waist. "Welcome home, Mrs. Rome," he said and her heart thudded and she wished with all her heart that they had a real marriage.

She struggled to let go of all worries about his cold heart in order to try to make this wedding night a thrilling memory, untainted by reality.

She wanted to love him, to have him make love to her, wondering if this night would be any better and not the disappointment that lovemaking had been in the past. She stood on tiptoe to kiss him.

His arms tightened around her, crushing her to him

while she combed her fingers into his thick mass of curly hair and wrapped her other arm around his neck. Leaning over her, he kissed her possessively, groaning with longing, his tongue a slow, hot exploration.

She thrust her hips against him, knowing they could take hours, certain he was the kind of consummate lover that would be deliberate, tantalizing, infinitely sexy.

Each kiss and caress heightened her appetite for him. She poured herself into her kisses, wanting to obliterate the stream of women that must have been in his life.

Shoving away his jacket, she unfastened the studs of his shirt. His fingers tangled in her hair, sending pins flying and he combed out her long locks slowly while he continued to kiss her.

She pushed away his shirt and ran her hands across his broad shoulders, sliding them down to tangle in his soft, dark chest hair. She freed him of his trousers that fell away.

As she traced kisses over his muscled stomach, he groaned and lifted her to her feet. Unzipping her dress and pushing it away, he held her hips while lust darkened his expression.

He stood in his low-cut, narrow briefs that couldn't contain him while he looked at her leisurely, a heated gaze that was as tangible as a caress.

"You're gorgeous," he whispered, unfastening the clasp to yank away her lace bra. Cupping her breasts in his hands, he rubbed his thumbs over her nipples lightly in an enticing torment.

She gasped, gripping his narrow waist and closing her eyes while streaks of pleasure streamed from his touch.

"This is a dream," she whispered, winding her fingers in his thick curls as he bent down to take her nipple in his mouth, to kiss and suck and tease, his tongue circling where his thumb had been.

"No dream," he said, the words coming out slowly as his ragged breathing was loud. Hooking his thumbs in the narrow band of her thong and her pantyhose, he peeled them away and she stepped out of the last of her underclothes. He held her hips again, straightening and leaning away to look at her as she stood naked before him.

"I've waited too long for this moment," he whispered.

"There should be more to it," she whispered, unable to refrain from letting her bitterness slip about this loveless night. If he heard, he didn't acknowledge it. She peeled away his briefs and he stepped out of them, leaning down to pull off his socks.

As he straightened he picked her up and she raised her face to his, winding her arms around his neck, without looking to see where he carried her.

Still kissing her, he placed her on the bed. He was astride her and he leaned over to shower kisses to her breasts, his tongue stroking each pouty bud. His fingers drifted across her belly, down over her thigh and then so lightly, back up between her thighs. Her cry was loud in the silence, the tantalizing need building in her. Matt was loving her and she could make love to him in return, man and wife for tonight at least.

Reaching to caress him, she opened her legs to him. She kept her eyes closed as Matt explored and teased slowly, his caresses feathery touches, his tongue hot and wet, her need intensifying swiftly.

Driving away her thoughts about a loveless union, he moved lower, raining kisses down the inside of her leg, holding her foot as he caressed her and his hands played over her. Beneath his touch, she arched her hips and writhed.

His muscled thighs were covered in short, curly black hairs that gave slight friction against her skin.

"Turn over," he whispered, rolling her over without waiting. And then he moved between her legs, his fingers playing over her, touching, caressing and exploring, discovering where he could touch to get the biggest response from her. His tongue followed where his fingers had been and when he slipped his hands along the inside of her thighs, sliding higher until he touched her intimately, she gasped and attempted to roll over, but he placed his hand in the middle of her back.

"Lie still, Brianna," he ordered, his fingers driving her to dig her fists into the bed and spread her legs wider.

She moaned, crying out, attempting to turn until finally he allowed her to and then his hand was back between her thighs, touching, rubbing, exploring, another constant tease.

Losing all awareness of anything except his hands and mouth on her, she arched wildly, spreading her legs so he had full access to her.

"Brianna, love, you're beautiful!" he gasped, but she barely heard what he said and paid no heed. She had to have him inside her, wanting his heat and hardness.

With a cry, she raised her hips higher. "Love me!" she gasped as she fell back and he kissed her deeply. She returned his loving, but then pushed him away and down on the bed to climb astride him and pour kisses down across his belly as she stroked his hard rod.

She shifted to take him in her mouth, her tongue circling the velvet tip while he clenched his fists in her hair and groaned, letting her kiss and caress him for minutes until he sat up suddenly to pull her to him and lean over her, kissing her thoroughly.

She kissed him in return until he placed her on the bed and started the loving anew, his hands playing over her lightly, caressing while her need climbed to a fever pitch.

He moved between her legs, hooking them over his shoulders to give him access to her as he kissed and stroked her.

Her eyes fluttered open and she saw him watching her when she gasped with gratification.

"Do you like this?" he whispered, his tongue flicking over her and she moaned softly.

"Yes, yes," she whispered, caressing his strong thighs, stroking his manhood. "Love me, Matt," she whispered, placing her hands on his hips, to tug him closer as he continued to caress and kiss her.

When he moved between her legs and she opened her eyes to look at him, her heart thudded with longing. He was handsome male perfection, ready and poised. Tangles of black curls fell on his forehead and his face was flushed. His body was lean, hard muscles and his manhood thick and ready.

She held her arms out to him. "Love me, Matt. Become part of me."

He lowered himself, wrapping an arm around her as he kissed her passionately again.

Slowly, he entered her, the hot, hard tip of his manhood plunging into her softness, making her cry out with longing. Still kissing her, he withdrew. His kiss muffled her cry as he entered her again, hot and slow, filling her and withdrawing, tempting and stirring desire to white heat.

The teasing heightened enjoyment while driving her wild with wanting him to love her, reaching a point she'd never known where she was desperate for his loving.

She tore her mouth from his. "Matt, I want you!" she cried, arching against him, her hands sliding over his firm bottom trying to draw him closer, her legs tightening around his waist.

He entered her slowly and she moved beneath him, and then they rocked together.

With her blood thundering in her ears and her eyes squeezed tightly closed, she held him, crying out for him to keep loving her. When she climaxed, spasms shook her and ecstasy consumed her. Lights burst behind her closed eyelids and she couldn't stop moving with him until she climaxed again and heard him cry her name.

As she clung to him, he thrust wildly in her. Enjoyment she'd never known before rippled with aftershocks of pleasure.

Finally, they quieted, their ragged breathing returning to normal as he showered light kisses on her face and shoulders and murmured endearments she couldn't believe.

Turning his head, he kissed her fully on the mouth, a long, slow kiss of gratification. They had shared the time with a mutual pleasure but love was missing. Even though he acted like a man in love, she knew he wasn't.

Holding him close, she caressed him while they continued to kiss until finally he raised his head. "You were worth the wait, Brianna. My decision is justified."

Once again he focused on himself, reminding her she was locked into a businesslike bargain. "I can say the same." She was unwilling to think beyond the present moment.

This time with him was fleeting and false. On the plus side, if they had been wildly in love, she couldn't imagine they would have had better sex. He truly was the consummate lover she had expected.

Finally, holding her close against him, he rolled onto his side.

"I don't want to let you go. I can't believe my good fortune in finding you," he whispered.

"I suppose we can both feel fortunate," she said lazily, enjoying being held in his arms and feeling euphoric, trying to keep at bay all the hurt over the lack of love in their relationship, yet feeling an emptiness behind the pleasure.

His hands played lightly over her and he showered kisses on her temple, throat and ear, all faint touches that rekindled her desire.

"Ah, Brianna, you're the best," he murmured, yet

she paid little heed, assuming he was repeating what he'd said before. Deep inside, along with desire for sex, was a hungry need for a true relationship that she couldn't dissolve. She should be more like Matt and focus on the money involved in this arrangement, but it was turning out almost from the first that she couldn't.

"Come here, darlin'," he said, leaning down to scoop her into his arms. Wrapping her arms around him, she combed locks of his hair off his forehead.

"Where are you taking me?" Without waiting for his answer, she pulled him closer to kiss him.

When he raised his head, he crossed the room with her and entered a huge bathroom that held a sunken tub. Matt set her on her feet and turned spigots. "We'll bathe together," he said, testing the water and then turning to pick her up again and carry her into the tub.

Setting her on her feet, he kissed her while water rose and swirled around their legs. Finally, he stopped and took her into his arms again to sit down, holding her close against him.

"You've got an insatiable appetite," she whispered. She could feel his manhood, thick and hard and ready for her again.

"What can I say? You make my blood boil."

"I can do something about that right now," she said in a sultry voice, turning and sitting astride him to lower herself onto him. Desire ignited again, a hungry need that she couldn't believe had been so totally satisfied only a short time earlier, yet now she wanted him with a desperation that seemed fiercer than ever.

He kissed her as she moved on him and in minutes she cried out when she climaxed and felt him shudder from his own orgasm.

Soon she was seated between his legs in a tub of hot, swirling water.

"Better and better," she murmured and felt a rumble in his chest when he laughed softly.

"Before the night is over I'll show you better and better," he promised and her pulse jumped at the prospect.

"This is temporary," she said without thinking.

"Shh," he commanded. "It's not temporary tonight and it won't end anyway, not until we want it to end."

"Until you want it to end," she corrected. "But no matter. Tonight I don't want any angst. This is the best ever," she said, trying to ignore that nagging inner voice.

When they climbed out and toweled each other dry, as she lightly rubbed the soft terry cloth over his body, she looked into his hungry blue eyes. A flame started low inside her.

While he continued to watch her, he rubbed her nipples lightly with a dry towel. Then his towel slipped between her legs as he stroked her.

She gasped, closing her eyes, and he tossed aside his towel to pull her closer, one arm circling her waist and his other hand stroking her soft feminine bud while he kissed her.

In minutes she had her eyes squeezed tightly shut as she held him and moved, his hand driving her wild.

"Matt, I want your love," she said, meaning it literally, knowing he would think only in terms of passion.

He picked her up to carry her to bed and finish what he'd started. Midmorning while they lazed in each other's arms in bed, he combed her hair from her face with his fingers. Caressing his chest, she curled the tight hairs around her forefinger.

"Matt, I'm beginning to have hunger pangs. I think the meal yesterday on the plane was the last time we ate."

"Could be," he drawled in a lazy, satisfied voice. "The only hunger I have is for you," he said, his voice thickening as he rolled on his side and gazed at her. "A penny for your thoughts."

"You'd have to pay a lot more than that. Besides, you can probably guess my thoughts," she drawled in a throaty tone and saw his eyes darken. Could he possibly surmise what she was contemplating, or what she really wanted? If she could, would she trade his money for his love? The question came out of the blue and was one she didn't want to pursue. Why did it matter so much to her? Yet she knew exactly why, and the closer she drew to him in physical intimacy, the more she wanted an emotional relationship. Love was never part of the equation, she reminded herself.

He drew his finger along the top of the sheet where it curved over her breasts, a faint touch that stirred tingles and aroused her again.

She caught his hand. "You wait. You're going to have to feed me before you have me again, mister."

"You think?" he asked, sounding amused. "There's a challenge that I might have to rise to."

"You've already risen and you need to cool it," she

said, knowing she was fighting a battle she didn't even want to win. "How easily you can manipulate me," she said. "Shameless!"

"I'll show you shameless," he retorted, rolling her onto her back and moving over her to lick and kiss until she forgot about food and only wanted him.

"Matt, come here!" she cried, pulling him over her and wrapping her long legs around his waist.

He lowered himself into her, thrusting hard and fast this time as she rose to meet him.

With another burst of satisfaction, she climaxed. Rapture enveloped her while she continued to move with him until he climaxed and called out her name.

"Brianna! Love! My love!"

She knew the endearments were meaningless and she should ignore them, but for today, she relished knowing he wanted her.

Later, she curled against him in his arms with her hair spilling across his chest. She could hear the steady beat of his heart, feel the rhythmic thumping beneath her hand. She was satiated, lethargic.

"I can't move," she whispered, running her forefinger in slow circles through his thick chest hair.

"We'll bathe and then go eat."

"I think we had the same plans earlier, but they went awry. Perhaps we shouldn't bathe together this time."

"Perish the thought. A simple bath and food. The simplicities of life."

"It doesn't seem to work out that way. This time, I'll tip the scales in favor of getting to eat," she said and slipped out of bed, gathering a sheet around her as she hurried away from him to the bathroom to shower alone. She locked the bathroom door behind her, certain if he came and pounded on it, she would open it at once.

To her surprise, he let her go and she showered and dried in total silence. Wrapping herself in a thick maroon towel, she went to find him.

She located Matt with glasses of orange juice, a pot of coffee, a tall glass of milk and covered dishes, some on the table and some still on a nearby cart. He wore jeans and a T-shirt and his hair was wet.

She walked up behind him to slide her arms around his waist. "You're a fast cook."

"I used my powers of persuasion to get room service to deliver on the double. Now feast away, my love. I ordered everything I could think you might like."

His "my love" stung. She wasn't his "love" and it bothered her more than she'd expected it would. She tried to focus on all she was gaining, but love was turning out to be far more important than she'd expected.

With her appetite suddenly diminished, she sat down, opening dishes and discovering tempting omelets, scrambled eggs, hot biscuits, slices of ham, strips of bacon, bowls of strawberries and a fruit plate with grapes, melons and pineapple slices.

"This is the ideal way to start the day," he said, and his tone took her attention from food. She looked up to see him seated, watching her with his head propped on his fist.

"Aren't you going to eat?" she asked.

"Yes, but I was thinking about last night."

She waved her fork at him. "Do not think lusty thoughts until I've had breakfast. I really forbid it!"

"Yes, ma'am, sexy wench."

She laughed. "Not really. What's our schedule?"

"Tomorrow we fly to Rome," he said.

"I hope I see it. I haven't seen anything of New York City. Not even the park, which is right across the street."

"We'll be back here soon, I promise. Then I'll take you anywhere you want to go."

She set down her fork and took a drink of milk. "You've given me paradise and allowed me to do things I could only dream about before."

"It's a good arrangement," he said. She hoped she hid her disappointment, because he could have been discussing a business transaction he'd made.

In minutes she forgot her disappointment as she returned to eating breakfast, determined to get a glimpse of Central Park before he carried her back to bed.

With each passing mile of their flight to Rome, Matt was pleased to see she was captivated. She hovered at the window, looking at little more than clouds and water, yet she seemed totally engrossed. "Flying is the best possible means of travel!" she said.

"If you'll save all that enthusiasm until we're in bed, this will really be a memorable day."

She smiled. "I'll remember this flight always," she said, and he wondered how long they would stay together. Right now, he was unable to imagine tiring of her, but he always eventually grew bored with women. Yet he suspected Brianna would last longer than any of the others ever had.

"I'll bring you back plenty of times, Brianna, so you'll be able to fly more often than you'll want. You'll see Europe to your heart's content."

"I can't envision such a thing. You take this for granted. Even if I moved here to live, I can't imagine ever being that way."

"You'll be a jaded traveler, I promise."

"Don't make promises you can't keep. We'll never know who's right, but I feel certain I am."

"I'll tell you what I want—I want you in my arms in bed."

"Later, later," she said, waving her fingers at him without tearing her gaze from outside the window. "I want to see everything."

"I figured you would," he answered with amusement. "Enjoy it. Rome will be more fascinating than ocean and clouds."

"I'm scared to even think about Rome," she said.

"You—scared? I don't believe it. You'll be fine, and as my wife, you'll be totally accepted."

"I want to see as much as possible in the short time we'll be there."

"I'll repeat—I promise to bring you back, so you don't have to try to see and do everything this time," he said. He suspected he was going to have to do the tourist things sometime this week for her sake, but he'd be thinking about how he couldn't wait to make love again.

* * *

In Rome, they moved into a luxurious suite in the hotel where Matt usually stayed. She gawked only slightly at the elegant lobby, and then they were locked in their suite and could have been in a tent as far as the outside world was concerned.

Matt had intended to show her Rome, but his intentions were lost in lovemaking until Friday, when he left her a limo and driver while he attended a meeting.

She had a whirlwind tour, stopping at the Colosseum and at St. Peter's. As she stood in St. Peter's Square and admired the beauty of the ancient Basilica, she thought how some of her dreams had become empty and disillusioning.

All through the years of growing up with hardships and only hopes of becoming affluent, and then through the generous bargain with Matt, she had thought riches would give her all she wanted. Matt's money would give her, her baby and her family comfort, education and security—but the rest was empty.

She had been thrilled over the prospect of a honeymoon in Rome, but now that she was here, it was not the pleasure she had expected. She wished she had someone with her to share each discovery—there would be no great memories to take home from this trip. She'd brought her camera, yet she didn't care to keep any pictures. Love was missing and it made a difference.

The real disappointment was Matt. There were moments he was charming company. How easily she could fall in love with him if only—

She stopped that train of thought. Matt was who he was, and she had to accept it. He was at a meeting today, working to get even more wealth. Yet she had been guilty, too, of placing too much importance on money.

She stood in the square, combing her breeze-tussled hair away from her cheek with her fingers, and realized she would never feel quite the same about what was truly important in life.

Strolling around, she only half looked at her surroundings, still lost in her thoughts and hurting because she had locked herself into a situation where she lived with a charming man who didn't even know she existed except in bed.

Finally, she turned away to head back to the limo, wanting to stop her sightseeing for the day, wondering if she would ever return to Rome with someone she loved.

Later in the afternoon, Matt arrived, sweeping in the door and kicking it closed as he pulled her into his embrace.

"How did you like Rome?" he asked, and her half-hearted answer was lost in his kisses, her sightseeing report forgotten.

Getting ready for the charity ball, Brianna took her things to the large bathroom. She knew Matt had already showered and was dressing which would take him no time. When she finished bathing, she expected to have the bedroom and bathroom to herself. She didn't want distractions from Matt while she got ready and she con-

tinually ran through the list of names of the investors
and facts about them.

As she dressed, she wondered if Matt had concerns
about his new wife's inexperience. So far, he'd ex-
pressed absolutely none. She felt as if anyone could
glance at her and sense her background, her lack of
experience and sophistication, yet she reminded
herself that Matt's monumental self-assurance would
cover a lot.

Repeatedly during the trip, she had been thankful for
the honeymoon being in Italy and the ball being in
Rome, because for the past two years she had been
studying Italian in college. Since she felt she might be
interested in international law, she wanted a minor in
languages. The day she learned about the ball, she'd
even gone out and bought a crash course in "Teach
Yourself Conversational Italian" to practice further.

Finally, she went to find him at his desk, poring over
something. The desk light caught glints in his thick
black hair. She wondered how he could tune out the
world and concentrate on business when he had only
minutes before leaving for a glamorous evening with
people he intended to impress. Her palms were damp
with nervousness and she felt the same as she had on
the first job interview in Cheyenne.

"Matt," she said softly.

"One minute, Brianna," he answered, his head still
bent over figures. "I want one more minute to finish this
list," he said. "I'm in the middle of—" His words died
as he glanced up at her and he stared at her. "You're

gorgeous," he said, his voice becoming husky as it did when he was aroused.

She let out her breath. One hurdle passed. Her pulse speeded when he circled the desk toward her, never taking his gaze from her.

When he crossed the room, she tingled. Fighting the urge to smooth her skirt, she knew she was dressed as flawlessly as she could in a scarlet sleeveless dress that was the most expensive dress she'd ever owned with the exception of her wedding outfit. Cut in a low V neckline, the skirt split up one side to an inch above her knees and she wore matching sandals.

"You look too beautiful to waste the evening at a ball," he whispered, walking up to her and slipping an arm around her waist. As he leaned toward her, she pushed lightly against him, wiggled out of his embrace and stepped away.

"Not so soon. You don't know how long I worked to achieve this look. Let's go. When we return tonight, you can do as you please and I promise I won't protest."

He groaned. "You make things so difficult."

"You'll manage," she said, smiling at him while her pulse raced.

"Shall we go?" he asked, offering her his arm. She nodded and stepped close to loop her arm through his.

The streets of Rome were congested. Traffic was busy, and her case of nerves returned, but not as threatening as before because now she was at ease with Matt and he was the one person who mattered.

"This city is beautiful," she said, knowing this

night would remain a vivid memory for the rest of her life.

"Yes," he answered, smiling at her. "Did you enjoy the sights? I haven't heard about your day."

"Of course I did. I hope yours was successful— whatever your meeting was about."

"About an investment I have. Yes, I had a productive meeting. And now we're going to impress some people tonight," he said, still smiling.

"Rome seems incredibly noisy. Scooters are every-where," she said, barely aware of her statement, trying to stop reflecting on Matt's ambition.

"Here we are," he said. "I want you to have a mem-orable evening."

The limo halted in front of the canopied door of a luxury hotel where lights blazed. As she emerged, her nervousness climbed. She inhaled deeply, glancing at Matt, who looked drop-dead handsome in his tux. Smiling at her, he turned to hold her hand. Squaring her shoulders, she decided to simply enjoy herself and to stop worrying over the impression she might make.

Her heart twisted because he was still thinking about work and the investors.

They entered the large ballroom, where a waltz played and couples danced.

From the first moment in the door, Matt greeted people and introduced her to too many to recall. The names of the investors she finally had firmly in mind and within minutes she saw the first one approach. He was a tall, black-haired man with a beautiful black-haired woman was at his side. His dark gaze was on Brianna. "Here comes—"

"Signore Ruffuli and his wife, Letta," Brianna said quietly to Matt. "And his wife doesn't speak English."

"Very good!" Matt smiled broadly, turning to greet the couple.

"Buona sera, Signore Rufulli e Signora Rufulli," Matt acknowledged his friend and his wife. *"Vorrei presentarle a la mia sposa,"* Matt said in fluent Italian, turning to make introductions to Brianna.

"Buona sera, Signori Rufulli. Piaciere di fare la loro conoscenza. Che bella serata." Brianna smiled as she greeted them.

While the men talked, the two women conversed until Matt took her arm as they walked on to meet others.

"You surprised me," he said. "You didn't tell me you speak Italian."

"It's very limited. In college I had two years and I studied a little in one of those crash courses on a CD, 'Teach Yourself Conversational Italian,' before we came tonight."

"I'm impressed," Matt said as he gave her an appraising study and she wondered what he was thinking.

"I intended you to be," she said, turning to smile at a blond man who approached them and shook hands with Matt as he greeted him.

"Brianna, please meet Sven Ingstad. Sven, I want you to meet Brianna Rome."

"I hoped to meet your lovely wife," he said in a courtly manner while he smiled at her.

Gradually, they circled the fringe of the dance floor and she met all the men from the investment group who were present. She knew from beforehand that three wouldn't be present at the charity ball.

Finally, she was in Matt's arms to dance, and as they whirled across the floor, he studied her. "You have facets to you I know nothing about. I may have to reassess my expectations."

"If you think that, from my standpoint, the evening just became a success," she said, flirting with him.

"Then I think we can both count tonight as a big accomplishment. You've captivated them."

She laughed. "I hardly think 'captivated' is the correct description. I hope they like and approve of me," she said, refraining from adding that he was the one whose opinion of her was important.

"There isn't another man on this earth who wouldn't approve of you," Matt said, and his voice dropped a notch lower. "Wait and see, as the evening wears on, who wants to dance with you."

Except that approval by others was important to Matt, she hardly cared about his business acquaintances. Matt was pleased with her because it moved him closer to his goal, but she still had the feeling that he saw her only in those terms—and through desire. Matt never seemed to miss the women who had gone out of his life. Why did she expect to be different? Was there any way to break through that total focus he had on wealth and make him see her as part of his life? And since when had she started wanting to? Was she already falling in love with him in spite of fully knowing what he was like?

"How long do you think it will take before they invite you to join?" she asked.

"I can't answer that. I don't think they will for a couple of months at the earliest. Anxious for this marriage to end?" he asked and she wondered how much he was teasing and how serious he was.

"Not at all," she said. "Why would I be? I'm doing the Grand Tour. I don't want this to end."

"That wasn't the answer I hoped for," he said, gazing at her with a questioning speculation. "I wanted a reason that included me," he said and, again, she wondered at his statement.

"So do you want to hear that I think you're the sexiest man on earth and I can't wait to be back in bed with you?"

His blue eyes darkened. "The first possible moment, we're out of here," he said.

The music ended and Sven Ingstad appeared to ask her to dance, followed by another Italian acquaintance of Matt's who was widowed.

Wide doors were opened on an adjoining reception area where long tables were covered in fancy dishes of caviar, foie gras, truffles, brandied fruit, crepes, tempting chocolate extravaganzas and other exotic dishes she couldn't recognize. Throughout the evening, talking with wives, or in clusters of people she had met tonight, it was her tall, handsome husband who took her attention. Even when separated, she was aware of where he was, glimpsing him while he danced one time with each of the investors' wives and she knew he charmed each one and probably impressed on them how delighted he was to be married.

Most of his time was spent at her side; he poured the attention on her and she suspected it was for the benefit of those investors he hoped to convince that he was happy in his union. Who would think a man on his honeymoon wasn't wildly in love with his new wife? Whatever his motive, she enjoyed Matt's undivided attention, his flirting, his amusing anecdotes.

When the band took a break for an intermission, a dignitary stepped to the microphone and introduced the planners of the ball. Then awards were made to the six largest contributors and Matt was called forward to receive a plaque, which he placed on their table.

"Matt, that's terrific!"

He barely glanced at the plaque. "It was a good cause and it's tax deductible," he said and she guessed he contributed to impress the investors.

In a short time the band commenced playing again and Brianna was swept back up into the fray.

Later, dancing with Matt, Brianna was surprised to discover it was midnight. "The evening has flown, Matt. I'll always remember this night and every detail of it."

"I'm glad. And I think we've stayed as long as newlyweds should be expected to. We're leaving," he said.

Her pulse jumped because as successful as the evening had been, the prospect of making love with Matt was vastly more exciting. She'd had her night in Rome, but now it was time to return to the privacy of their suite with a man who had to be the most fantastic lover possible.

Seven

When they were seated in the limousine and on the road with the partition to the front of the limo closed, Matt pulled her onto his lap.

"You were an asset tonight," he said, thinking she had been. She had surprised him and he was certain charmed many others. "I've been waiting to do this." He removed the pins from her hair and dropped them into his pocket.

Her green eyes were clear, fringed with thick black eyelashes, her lips full and soft. He wanted her with an intensity that seemed to increase each day.

"You wait until we get home. This is far too public and we might have to stop for some reason."

"I won't wait to kiss you," he said, knowing that would be an impossibility. For hours he had been ready to leave the ball, but he had known he should stay to shmooze with the investor group. He wanted them to know Brianna and to see that he was happily married.

He wondered if he would be invited into their group soon. If so, what about Brianna? He wasn't ready to dissolve their marriage. She was looking out the window of the limo, lost in her own thoughts. He toyed with long locks of her hair. "I haven't heard much about the places you went today. All you said was you enjoyed the sights."

"St. Mark's was beautiful." She studied him. "I'd guess that when you look at it, you are simply trying to estimate the value of it."

He smiled. "I'll have to admit, I've given thought to its monetary value because the amount would be staggering."

"Not to you. And if you could turn a profit, I think you'd go after even a famous landmark."

"Never a sacred one. No, I don't think I would. Usually, famous landmarks are national treasures or otherwise off-limits or not financially feasible. Is something bothering you?"

She gazed impassively at him. "Marriage, even a businesslike paper one, is complicated. Living with another person is a big change."

"I take it that's a convoluted yes. Is this because I haven't taken you sightseeing?"

She shook her head. "Just little adjustments. It's good between us, Matt," she said, smiling at him. "You know it is."

Puzzled, he appraised her. "It's spectacular between us," he answered.

"Watch out, you'll get accustomed to having me in your life," she said with a twinkle in her eyes, and he smiled at her.

"I know I want you here now for damn sure," he replied. "Don't tell me you're getting emotionally tied up in this marriage?" he asked.

"I know better than to do that," she answered easily, running her hand over his knee, and he forgot their discussion.

Matt wrapped his arms around her and nuzzled her neck. She smelled sweet and was soft and he wished they could get home faster because he wanted to take her to bed. He raised his head to gaze into her eyes, seeing desire dance in their depths.

"Brianna," he said and she looked into his eyes. He leaned the last few inches to kiss her, a long, lingering kiss that she returned with fire.

"This damn drive is too long," he said, once, and then bent to kiss her again. His fingers sought her zipper, but she caught his wrist.

"I'll remind you. We wait until we get back to our suite. This limo isn't the place."

"It is for me," he said. "I'll do what you want, but once we're in our suite, then I get my way." He pulled her close, cradling her head against his shoulder as he returned to kissing her.

The moment they entered their suite, he caught her to pull her into his embrace.

"Now, beautiful, I get to make long, slow love to you." He kissed her again and stopped thinking.

* * *

Around noon the next day, Matt gave Brianna a list of stores she might like and she left in the limo to go shopping.

The phone rang and he answered to hear Zach's voice.

"We acquired the property you wanted in Chicago," his friend said. "The contract is on your desk and you can sign when you return. They know you're on your honeymoon."

"Good."

"How'd the ball go?"

"How do you think? She wowed them," he answered without waiting for Zach's reply. "She was stunning, brilliant, charming the investors. She even conversed in Italian."

"I'm glad," Zach said. "Matt, if I'm wrong, I'll admit it. You know that. Maybe I underestimated her."

"I think you did," Matt said quietly.

"Be funny if you fall in love with the little woman."

Matt laughed. "No danger. And the 'little woman' has her own plans for the future."

"Sure," Zach said as if Matt had stated that Brianna could fly to Mars. "No morning sickness?"

"Nothing. If I hadn't heard her talk about her doctor's appointment, I wouldn't believe that she's pregnant. It doesn't show yet even slightly and she feels great. She's pumped up about the travel because she's never been anywhere, so that makes it fun."

"Will wonders never cease," Zach muttered.

"Matter of fact, Zach, see if you can clear my calendar next week. I think we'll stay longer. We might as well take one more week."

"Am I talking to Matthew Rome?" Zach asked, suddenly sounding puzzled.

"You heard what I said. Clear my calendar and I'll be in touch. Let me know if anything urgent develops."

He broke the connection and waited with his hand on the phone, lost in thought about Brianna and the night before. His gaze went to the empty bed and he wished she were still here. He wanted her as if they'd never made love. He couldn't concentrate on business for thinking about her, and he was thankful he'd taken another week off, but he wanted her back in his arms immediately. Recalling their conversation on the drive back to the hotel from the ball, he reflected on her warning to watch out, that he might get accustomed to having her in his life.

He gazed into space, wondering if such a thing could happen. And her remarks about her sightseeing had carried a slightly jarring undercurrent. It was obvious she recognized his life was focused on making profitable deals. He had more money than he could spend, but he liked the challenge of competing and acquiring lucrative assets. When she agreed to this marriage, she had known that much about him. So why would it disturb her now…unless she was becoming accustomed to his commitment and wanted it to continue?

His entire being was dedicated to acquisition and success. If she couldn't cope with that, she knew the conditions of the bargain she'd made.

Tossing aside worries about their relationship, he swore softly and looked at his watch, counting the hours until he'd be alone with her. His cousins, Zach, no one close seemed to think it was going to work out between them in this temporary marriage. Ridiculous. His union with her was already dizzying in its success, and any negative feelings on her part were insignificant. Her slight disapproval of his lifestyle would have no effect. Yet even as he came to that conclusion, he had an uncustomary ripple of dissatisfaction. Surely he wasn't getting bothered because he didn't have her one hundred percent approval. He refused to consider such a possibility.

On Saturday, daily life returned as they flew home, only her real life had changed forever. The first of the following week she spent two days drifting around his mansion while Matt flew to Houston to work and by the third day, she had already looked into online courses for next year. She was restless, bored and didn't have a circle of friends who had time on their hands.

Within five minutes after Matt returned home Friday night, they were naked, making love and she forgot boredom and loneliness.

The next morning she was in his arms listening to business deals he had transacted while he was away.

"Matt, you talk about your Texas ranch and property in Houston and Dallas, your property in Chicago and New York, and your Wyoming ranch. Other than the block your office is in here in Cheyenne, do you own any other Cheyenne property?"

"No. There's never been any particular reason to want any."

"I'd think you'd want to invest in more in Cheyenne since you live here. It's sort of an investment in the future."

"You might be right," he drawled in a lazy voice as he combed his fingers through her long hair. "I'll get someone to look into it."

"There are some old areas that could be fixed up and utilized and you have a lot of interest in cowboy life— it might be nice if you'd look into building a museum."

"I'll think about it. You look into museums and see what we have. I don't even know. Here's what I'm far more interested in," he said, his hand drifting along her slender throat and then lower.

"There's something else I want to discuss with you. While you were gone I looked into some online courses for next year." His hand stilled.

"I thought we'd settled the school situation. You'll go back after we part ways."

"You were gone three days. You'll be away a lot on business. I've worked all my life since I was eleven years old. I'm bored just sitting around here."

"There are charity jobs you can do that will keep you as busy as a full-time job, if that's what you'd prefer. I don't want you tied into something where you can't travel with me. I'd think you'd want to travel with me when I go to Europe or interesting places."

"Whether you are in Europe or here, you work. But I have a lot of time on my hands until the baby comes and charity work—a little will go a long way. Even after the baby is born, I'll have some time to myself and if I don't, I can drop the course. What's wrong with an online course if it doesn't interfere in any way with you?"

He rolled over to prop himself up on his elbow. His blue eyes had darkened and this time she recognized irritation. A muscle worked in his jaw that was thrust out stubbornly.

"We had an agreement. You're backing out of it and next thing I know, you'll be too involved in school to do what I want."

"I did agree. But I didn't realize how much time I'd have. I promise to drop classes instantly if they interfere in any way. Otherwise, what's it to hurt if I enroll?"

Scowling, he opened his mouth, but she put her finger over his lips. "You wait," she urged. "Think it over and then tell me your answer. If I make sure it doesn't interfere and you never even know I'm doing it, then what's the harm?"

"It's the principle."

She smiled. "That's ridiculous, Matt. That simply means you want your way in this whether it's sensible or not. You think about it calmly and rationally and then give me an answer. You have excellent judgment."

"How long am I supposed to give this thought?"

"How about until this time next week?" she suggested.

"Very well, but I can't imagine changing my feelings on it."

"We can both change our minds if it's mutually agreeable, don't you think?"

He glared at her. "All right, you get your way. I'll think about it."

"That's all I want you to do. And in order to keep you happy in the meantime," she said softly, running her hand down his smooth back and over his bare, hard bottom, letting her fingers play on him. "I'll do my utmost to please you," she whispered, wrapping one arm around his neck and pulling him closer as her tongue flicked out to trace his lower lip.

With a groan he rolled over on top of her, sliding one arm beneath her to hold her while he kissed her and ran his other hand along her bare thigh.

In minutes she knew his annoyance with her had vanished and she did her best to pleasure him until he rolled her onto her back again. Lowering himself between her legs to enter her, he filled her swiftly and then pumped as if driven and unable to take his time while she cried out with pleasure, moving with him.

Later, when they lay in each other's arms, he showered her with light kisses and caresses. "This is great, Brianna," he said.

"But not as great as a business deal and making money. You get a high from gaining more wealth, don't you?"

He studied her with a penetrating look. "Thank heaven I don't have to choose between sex or making money," he replied.

Solemnly, she shook her head.

As snow swirled and fell outside, they spent the weekend in bed together and Monday, the last week of October, when she kissed him goodbye, she had a pang because she was going to miss him badly.

Watching him drive away, she wondered if he would consider her enrollment in online courses. She thought he was being ridiculously stubborn simply because he wasn't accustomed to anyone telling him no or even giving him bad news, much less wanting to go back on a promise.

She hoped he thought about it. In the meantime, she had plans for now. Her entire family was coming to town and this time she would put them in the mansion.

It was time to get them enrolled in colleges or trade schools, as she'd intended. If they wanted to return to the life they'd had before, they always could, but she suspected each one of them would move on to something better than they'd had in the past.

She planned to talk to her mother and set up an account for her. She could afford it easily and she knew her mother was accustomed to a simple life and would keep confidential what Brianna did.

That night, she sat at the large informal table in the breakfast dining area and gazed around the table while everyone ate and talked. Her mother sat at the other end of the table and was talking to Brianna's youngest sister, Danielle. She watched Danielle laugh, her eyes sparkling while she and their mother took turns helping Emma and Hunter, Danielle's children.

"I still think this bubble will burst and I'll find out it never was true," Melody said.

"It's very true," Brianna replied. "Matt has been liberal with my allowance and about letting me do what I want to do," she said, having no intention of telling any of them the actual situation at this point. So far as she could tell, both her family and Matt's had accepted their marriage and thought they were in love, which suited her fine.

Through the weekend and into the next week, they pored over college catalogs, made calls, sent e-mails and contacted schools, searching for places for her relatives to attend school. All the men except her youngest brother enrolled in the University of Wyoming. Both sisters had picked two-year schools in Laramie, solving their search quickly and were looking for places to live in Laramie.

Wednesday night as they all sat in one of the large recreation rooms, Matt called and said he'd arrived in town and was on his way home.

Brianna excused herself and met him at the door when he came in. Snow dusted his topcoat and flakes melted in his hair, drops glistening in the light. He stomped his booted feet.

Rushing to throw herself into his arms, she pulled him close for a long, heated kiss.

Finally he raised his head. "What are all the cars out there? Do we have company?"

"Yes, as a matter of fact—"

"Damn, I've been waiting to get home to you. Who's here and when are they leaving?"

"Actually, they're not leaving for a while. My family is here. I invited them and I'm getting them enrolled in colleges."

"Brianna, they're not *living* with us, are they? You have a nice family, but I don't want them underfoot while they get an education."

"I know you don't," she replied coolly, stepping away from him. "They came when you were away."

"I'm back and they're here now."

"They are. If I remember correctly, you are going out of town again Monday morning."

"Right. But my house is mine and I like solitude. I'll be glad to put them up in any hotel they want, but I want our house to ourselves."

"I hope you're not saying to get them out of here tonight," she said, growing angrier with him by the second. "It's snowing."

"No, I'm not," he replied with a long sigh. "But I hope you can have them moved when I return from the next trip."

"Matt, this is a huge, enormous mansion."

"Right. I like space, solitude and privacy. That's why few people have ever been here. I have guards, gates, high walls, a privacy fence and a gatekeeper. That's it, Brianna. I asked you to marry me. I did not marry your family or intend to share my home with them. Frankly, I'd feel the same about my own family."

"Matt, you're a coldhearted man with only one love."

"So be it. You knew that much when you married me. Your family goes. I can tell them or you can."

"I'll tell them because I can do it in a nicer way than you will."

"True enough. I hope you put them in a wing other than the one we're in," he stated, giving her an intent look.

"Of course I did. I could have hidden them in this castle, and you'd never even see them and you know it."

"Mentally, it isn't the same as having the place to myself."

"You are really unreasonable on this subject. I can't believe you would do this to your own family."

"I certainly would. Ask my dad which hotel he prefers. Enough said on that subject. I'll go greet them, but first, come here," he said, slipping his arm around her waist and drawing her to him to kiss her.

The minute his mouth touched hers, her annoyance with him evaporated. She kissed him in return.

Finally, she pushed away. "Right now, I'll admit, I wish we were alone. But I'm not tossing my family into the cold in the middle of the night."

"I didn't ask you to do any such thing. Come on and I'll go see the family," he said in a resigned voice and she shook her head.

"Heartless cad," she said under her breath, and he turned to smile at her.

"Although lovable, right?" he teased and she glared at him, but she knew she couldn't stay irritated with him. She could move her family and they'd be so excited over hotel life they wouldn't care. They'd probably think he was giving them a great welcome.

Matt charmed her mother and sisters. He played with her little nieces and nephews, counseled her brothers and brothers-in-law on schools and courses and performed a convincing act of enjoying being with everyone.

It was eleven o'clock when they finally closed the door to their bedroom suite and had complete privacy and hours later before she turned on her side to run her fingers over him while she talked to him.

"You charmed my family tonight, I'm sure. They don't have a clue you're the coldhearted reason they will be moved out."

"So be it, Brianna. A person knows what he wants."

"I'm reeling in shock from how nice you can act when actually, you're not in the least bit friendly."

"Your family isn't going to mind if you'll find a really fine hotel," he said, smiling at her.

"No, I know you're right. A hotel will be delightful for the little kids. Actually, all of them except Mom enjoy a pool."

"Your mom might, too. Buy her a swimsuit."

Brianna made a mental note to take her mother shopping.

"Come to town tomorrow and meet me for lunch."

"It's a date," she said.

The following day at eleven, Matt heard a small commotion outside his office door. His door swung open and Nicole entered his office a step ahead of Tiffany, who was protesting loudly. "I'm sorry, Mr. Rome," Tiffany said.

"Don't worry, Tiffany. It's fine," he said, although it wasn't fine at all and he didn't want to see Nicole.

As the door closed behind her, leaving them alone, Nicole smiled at him. "Don't be angry with her or with me. I was in the area and I thought I'd see if you wanted to do lunch."

"No, I don't. Or anything else, Nicole. I thought I made that clear last time we were together. My wife is meeting me soon and I'd as soon she didn't find you here in my office."

Still smiling, Nicole sat in a chair facing his desk. "Don't be such a bear. I'm sure she really doesn't care what you do. Come on, Matt. You and I know each other well and I know why you married. I also know you don't want me to talk to the press about it." She smiled at him.

"Don't try in any manner to blackmail or intimidate me," he said in a quiet, cold voice. "It isn't going to work."

"Sit down and relax, Matt," she said. "I seem to have a knack for picking the wrong days."

"Wait until you're invited and then you won't have that problem."

"I might have a long wait," she said, standing. Relieved that she looked as if she were going to leave, he lost some of his antagonism. He glanced at his watch.

"Don't worry about the little wife. She isn't going to raise too much of a fuss. I'm sure she never wants to go back to being a waitress."

"She won't ever have to do that," he said, waiting for Nicole to leave and aware of the passage of time. "Nicole, this is pointless. It's time for my appointment," he said, growing more impatient with her because he didn't want to have to explain her presence once again to Brianna. They'd had enough of a disagreement over her family at his house and she was due to arrive soon.

* * *

Brianna stepped off the elevator and a door opened. Zach emerged, stopping when he saw her. "Good morning."

"Hello, Zach," she answered coolly and hoped her wariness didn't show.

"You look very nice this morning."

"Thank you," she answered in a cold tone, waiting.

"I should admit to you that perhaps I made judgments too swiftly. I thought your marriage to Matt would be a disaster, but to the contrary, he seems happier than I've ever seen him. I think you're a good influence on him. It's only fair to tell you."

Surprised, she stared at him. She wondered if Zach actually meant what he was saying or if there was some ulterior motive. "Thank you," she answered quietly. "I'm glad to hear that, although marriage is a big uncertainty, whether it's one like ours or a real one."

He smiled at her. "I wanted you to know."

"Thank you," she reaffirmed cautiously, still wary of the turnaround in his views toward her. "I appreciate that and I hope you're right."

"I'm right about Matt. I've worked with him almost since the day he went on his own. Of course, life is filled with change and I know this is a temporary union. If you ever need me, call," he said, handing her his card.

"Thank you," she said again, more warmth in her voice this time. "A friend is always a good thing to have. I'll go now. I'm a little early, but I may as well get Matt and maybe we'll beat the lunch crowd."

"Brianna," he said, and she paused. "I heard you carried off the ball in Rome quite well and impressed Matt and others."

This time she gave him a full smile. "I'm glad to hear that," she said, feeling better and deciding Zach meant what he was saying. Surprised and pleased, she walked away.

The moment she stepped into Tiffany's office, she knew something was amiss. Tiffany's eyes widened and she knocked over a stack of books.

"Mrs. Rome," she said.

"Please, Tiffany, call me Brianna," she said patiently, wondering how many times she was going to have to ask his secretary before she would relax and address her by her first name.

She headed toward his office. "Is he in his office?"

"Yes, he is. If you'll wait, I'll announce you."

"You don't need to, thanks," she said, wondering what was the matter with Tiffany, who was growing more flustered and nervous as she crossed the room. Had Zach merely been trying to stall her, too? Brianna knocked and opened the door, coming face-to-face with Nicole Doyle.

Eight

"I'm going now," Nicole said, smiling broadly at Brianna.

She glanced past Nicole at Matt, who approached her with impassive features but blazing blue eyes. "Nicole is leaving, Brianna. Come in," he said, taking his wife's arm and brushing a kiss on her lips lightly. He draped his arm across her shoulders.

"Goodbye, Nicole. Please close the door as you go," he added in a cold tone.

Blowing him a kiss, she left, closing the door behind her.

Brianna couldn't keep from being annoyed, but common sense told her that it had to be like the last time.

"I didn't know she was coming," he explained.

"Then we'll drop the subject. I have a feeling if you wanted her around, I'd never have seen her at all."

He smiled, kissing her lightly. "Thanks and you're right. You're the woman for me, and I'm busy trying to get you to myself before I leave town."

When she chuckled, his smile faded. "You look gorgeous today, except when you entered my office, I wished there was absolutely nothing beneath that leather coat."

"In this weather?" She laughed. "It's a cold November day and I'm not visiting your office naked beneath my coat."

"I can still imagine. Let's have lunch," he said, taking her arm. "I want you. If we go home, your relatives are all over the place. This office is as private as the street outside."

"It's difficult to work up a lot of sympathy since we made love half the night last night. Besides, I'd guess you have appointments later today and we should have lunch and let you get on with your work."

In his secretary's office, she paused. "Tiffany, what time does he have to be back?"

"Actually, not until two o'clock."

"Thank you," Brianna said sweetly, smiling up at him. "We should go before every restaurant gets crowded."

She left with him, noticing Nicole's perfume still lingering in the air and wondering how persistent Nicole would be in trying to get back into Matt's life. And how successful.

When they were in his car, Matt watched the road. "Brianna, have you told your family about moving?"

"Not yet. You're leaving Monday and you'll be gone the rest of the week. I'll tell them then and they'll be gone when you return."

"Not sooner?"

"I'm afraid not. That would be difficult."

"How difficult to make a hotel reservation? I can do it and they'll like it."

She didn't answer and rode the short distance to the restaurant in silence, wondering about him and how solitary he was and how little he seemed to care for anyone else or anything else except money.

When they were seated in the restaurant and had ordered, she took off her coat and looked up to see Matt watching her and desire had ignited in his gaze. A tingle jolted her from her reverie and made her aware of her tight-fitting, plain navy sweater and skirt.

"You look gorgeous as usual. If I didn't have that appointment—"

"But you do," she finished. "I'll make you a deal. If you're not going to let my family stay at your house, the least you can do is help my brothers by giving them job advice. You have a lot of contacts, so you should know places to send them."

Matt groaned. "Brianna, I don't do job placement. I pay people who work for me to deal with hiring."

"Then it will be a good experience for you and broaden you to look beyond yourself a little. You're kicking them out of your house—so this is the least you can do," she persisted, knowing she was badgering him, but determined to get him to help her family.

"I didn't help my brothers—Lance works for me, but that was different, and Christopher is off playing football and doesn't give a rip what I'm doing. Your family will manage. Heaven knows, you do."

"They will manage much better with your help and you owe them."

"I don't think I owe them anything when I'm footing a giant hotel bill for six adults and four little kids."

"The little kids cost nothing. Now look, Matt, your mansion will easily hold all of them and they can stay out of your sight."

"Don't go back to that. They're out and I'll get Zach to look into helping them with jobs. How's that?"

She only hoped Zach would do his best for them. "I hope Zach will," she said, wondering whether he would actually help or merely go through the motions. He had seemed sincere in his compliments to her, but she didn't know him well, so she had no idea if he had been truly sincere.

As Matt drove, she stared at his long, lean frame and knew she was falling in love with him. He had been good to her and kind and generous to her family. He was the most fantastic lover. She thought she'd be able to guard her heart so easily and never fall in love with him because she still thought he was heartless when it came to work and money. And whatever happened, their union was temporary. She had no illusions about Matt changing his mind regarding the length of their marriage.

* * *

True to his word, Matt talked to some of her family about their future plans and gave them his business card, telling them to call his office to set up appointments to talk to Zach, who would help direct them where to turn in applications and resumes. Also, Zach would see about having their resumes professionally done, something Brianna had planned on doing herself, but she was relieved to see Matt take this on.

Again, that night when they finally were alone in the east wing of the house and closed in their bedroom, she wound her arms around his neck. "Thank you for today and all you're doing."

"If I can keep you happy and showing me how grateful you are," he said in a husky voice, "it's worth it to me."

"I wish you didn't have to go Monday and be gone so long. I'll miss you."

"I miss you more each time we're apart," he said.

"Have you ever thought about not traveling quite so much?" she asked, knowing even before she finished her sentence that business came far ahead of everything else.

"I'm doing what I have to do, but it's not quite the same," he said in a solemn tone that made her heart miss a beat. Could she possibly be growing more important to him?

He tightened his arms around her, leaning down to kiss her, and ending conversation and her curiosity.

* * *

Monday she kissed him before he left for Chicago and then she turned her attention to her family. As she had expected, news of the hotel move excited her family.

She began to plan a nursery, drawing sketches and studying magazines. Her pregnancy still seemed unreal to her because she couldn't see any change in her shape. Trying to stay fit, most days of the week she walked on Matt's track in his exercise room and swam in his indoor pool.

If she could take even two courses each semester, she would get four out of the way in a year. She was a senior and needed eighteen more hours for an undergraduate degree. She suspected after a few months, Matt wouldn't care what she did. His fascination with her would surely dwindle and she could take more than two.

She looked into some local charities that she could give a day to and miss when Matt wanted her to go with him, finally agreeing to give a day each week to helping in the local food bank.

When it was nearly ten o'clock Friday evening, Matt arrived. She'd spent the late afternoon and early evening getting ready for his return and had her black hair pinned up on either side of her head, to fall freely down on her back and on her shoulders. She'd selected new red silk lounge pajamas and matching high-heeled sandals and her excitement mounted with each passing hour. They'd talked half a dozen times during the day and she knew he was anxious to get home. Her pulse rate increased when she heard the beep of the alarm as a door opened and closed.

She rushed to meet him when he swept into the hallway bringing cold air with him. At the sight of him, her heart thudded even faster.

Dropping his briefcase, he shook off his thick, black topcoat and let it and his charcoal suit jacket fall on the floor with his briefcase. Hurrying toward her, he shed his tie.

She ran the last distance to throw her arms around him and he caught her up, crushing her in his embrace and kissing her hotly.

Beneath his cotton shirt and wool pants she could feel the warmth of his body. Running her fingers through his tangled curls, she kissed him. As her heartbeat speeded, her desire was a blazing fire. "I've missed you so!" she gasped and returned to kissing him.

"Not anything like the way I've missed you, Brianna," he declared. "Love, you look luscious enough to eat," he said and kissed her, scooping her into his arms to carry her to the bedroom.

Saturday she lazed in his arms. "Matt, look at the sun coming through the windows. It has to be midmorning. I have things to do, and so do you."

"You're complaining?"

She rolled on top of him, smiling at him. "Hardly. I'm euphoric and lusty, but I need to eat for the baby."

He smiled as he wrapped locks of her hair around his fingers and pulled her to him to kiss her.

His cell phone rang and he continued to kiss her until she broke it off. "Answer your phone. Only a select few have your cell phone number."

"It better be important," he grumbled, picking up his phone and saying hello. In moments, he sat up and she rolled away, grabbing her robe and going to shower, guessing it was a business call. She dressed in jeans and a T-shirt and went to the kitchen to get breakfast.

Soon he joined her. He had showered and dressed in chinos and a tan knit shirt. His damp hair was in tight curls. His eyes were bright with excitement and she realized the phone call had been something that pleased him. As she poured orange juice, she said, "You look like that cat who caught the mouse. What's happened?"

"I'm meeting with four members of the investment group Tuesday, so I'll fly to France Monday. They all but told me outright they want me to join their group."

First she felt excitement that he had achieved his goal. That quick flash was replaced by cold fear that he would be through with her and ask her to pack and go.

"Congratulations!" she cried, hugging him, letting him have his moment and wanting to avoid any dissonance.

"It'll only be overnight, they said. Come with me. They told me to bring you along."

He continued talking about Paris, but the joy at hearing he wanted her along was immediately crushed. He was taking her because they'd told him to.

He leaned down to look her in the eyes. "Are you with me? Paris? You look like you're thinking about something else."

"No, I'm delighted for you, and yes, I want to go."

"You don't sound as if you really do. I'm not twisting your arm," he said, studying her.

Smiling, she hugged him. "I'm just wondering if you join their group now, if you'll tell me goodbye," she said, but that wasn't really what had made her joy disappear.

He hugged her. "Hardly," he said, winding his fingers in her hair and pulling her head back to gaze into her eyes. "I want you in my life for a lot longer," he said and kissed her.

And she intended to be, she thought as she kissed him in return. She would make him want her for a long, long time—long enough that he might not ever want her to go.

In spite of his all-important drive for wealth, she loved her handsome husband. She reminded herself no one was perfect, but Matt's flaw was a gigantic one that could affect everything he did.

She pushed away from him. "We should eat and then let me plan what I have to do to get ready."

"They're taking us to dinner Tuesday night and I'm sure it'll be a celebration dinner."

She shook her head over his exuberance and absolute confidence. "Matt, I've never known anyone who has the self-assurance you do. My word, you believe in yourself!"

"I suppose I do, but why else would they be calling and asking me to meet with them and bring you and plan on dinner? It stands to reason. Go buy a new dress and we'll stay Wednesday. I'll take you out for our own little celebration the following night."

She took a breakfast casserole from the oven. As

they ate, she listened to Matt talk about his plans, but her mind was still on their future together and if she was important to him in any manner other than as a means to get him into this group, or in his bed.

She realized he was telling her about problems at work with acquisitions he wanted and the difficulty he was having with one of his vice presidents, and she began to pay close attention, pushing aside her worries as she absorbed what Matt was saying.

It was three in the afternoon when he left for an errand and she went shopping for a dress for her Paris dinners.

She arrived back home before Matt and began to pack and sort through clothes, knowing Matt could take all of her time when he returned home.

She finally heard him at six-thirty when it was dark outside and a cold wind howled around the house.

He rushed inside and her heart thudded, desire instantly igniting because he looked irresistible. His broad-brimmed black hat was pushed to the back of his head and his thick leather and lambs-wool lined jacket swung open. He carried two huge boxes and she wondered if he'd purchased a suit for himself.

"So you've been shopping, too," she said. "I'd hug you, but I can't get close to you."

"Let's go to the family room," he said and, though he had four rooms the description would have fit, she knew which room was his favorite.

She already had a roaring fire blazing in the mammoth fireplace. She turned, waiting for him to set down his packages, and then she was in his arms and the world vanished.

It was hours later when she stirred and sat up in front of the fire. "I'm burning on one side, cold on the other and this floor is hard."

"It's not all that's hard and that's your fault," he said with amusement, pulling her to him to kiss her.

"Stop and let me move to higher ground. A bed and a warm shower first. And tonight, I get dinner at a decent hour. You know, it isn't healthy for a pregnant woman to miss meals."

Matt looked stricken. "Darlin', I'm sorry. I swear you won't miss another one—"

She placed her fingers on his mouth and smiled at him. "Stop. I feel fine. But food would be good right now."

"Steak it is. You go upstairs to shower and I'll shower in another bath and get dinner on the table."

Smiling at him, she left to do what he suggested. It wasn't until after dinner and they had moved back to the family room that she remembered his packages. He knelt to get the fire built up again, the scent of the burning logs filling the room. His jeans pulled tightly on his muscled legs and he straightened, setting the screen in place.

"Did you buy yourself a new suit?"

"I shouldn't have forgotten all about this," he said, picking up a long, narrow box that was the smaller of the two. He brought it to her to hand it to her.

"I should have had that sent out, but they were on the verge of closing and the truck had gone for today."

Curious, she opened the box to look at dozens of red and white and yellow roses. "Matt, these are gorgeous!" she said, taking out the card and pulling it open swiftly to read. "Thanks for helping me reach my goal. Love, Matt."

She set down the box and kissed him, pushing away from him in a moment.

"Wait now. I want to put these in water. They have them in those little vials, but I need to get them into a vase."

Rushing to get them in water before he tried to stop her, she had seen the look in his eyes and his thoughts weren't on the flowers.

He followed her into the kitchen, talking to her about Paris, and when she finished her arrangement in a large crystal vase, he carried it back to the family room for her.

As soon as he set it on a table, he crossed the room to pick up the largest box to give to her. It was tied with a red silk ribbon.

"I thought this was a suit for you," she said.

"They don't tie my suits up with silk bows. I have them custom-made by my tailor."

He placed the box on a leather sofa and she leaned down to untie a beautiful bow. She raised the lid and pushed away tissue paper to gaze at a box filled with dark fur.

Startled, she glanced at him.

"It's your present," he reminded her.

Burying her fingers in the soft, silky fur she lifted out a full-length mink coat. A card fell out and Matt picked it up off the floor to hand it to her. "Thank you, love, Matt."

"Matt, this is beautiful," she said, running her fingers through the thick fur. Yet instantly she wondered if the coat was a bribe to smooth the way and get her to go quietly when he told her they were through.

"It's elegant," she said, slipping it on, but feeling stiff and cold, knowing she should steel herself for what was to come. She turned to face him.

"You look gorgeous, but I really like you better with nothing," he said, smiling and walking up to slip his hands beneath the coat and wrap his arms around her.

Putting her arms around his neck, she stood on tiptoe to kiss him, a thorough, heated kiss. She wanted him and didn't want to be tossed out like old shoes, yet she couldn't believe that wasn't the exact reason for the gift.

She leaned away. "You don't even know for certain that they'll invite you to join. If they don't, do I lose my coat?" she asked in a teasing tone, trying to cover the chill she still suffered and the dread that had consumed her.

"You'll keep the coat no matter what, but I'm sure I'm in."

"Congratulations, again," she said quietly. "This is an extravagant gift."

"I want you to have it," he said, drawing her back into his embrace and leaning down to kiss her, yet even his hot kisses couldn't drive away the demons that tormented her.

Arriving in Paris late Monday afternoon, they checked in to another luxurious suite in a hotel near the Arc de Triomphe.

Matt had attributed her sober manner to jitters about dinner with the group of foreign investors and their wives again. Letting him continue to think that, she smiled politely at his reassurances that she shouldn't worry about Tuesday night.

While she unpacked in their bedroom, Matt walked up behind her and took clothes out of her hands.

"Stop working the instant you arrive. We have the rest of the day. I'll show you some sights and take you to dinner," he said, nuzzling her neck.

She turned to wrap her arms around him and kiss him passionately, still certain the mink coat had been a farewell gift and a bribe.

Matt's arms tightened around her, and sightseeing and her fears were all pushed aside.

After making love far into the night, they slept. Brianna woke after only a couple of hours and couldn't go back to sleep. She kept thinking about leaving Matt and it hurt. She loved him. There was no turning back and reversing her feelings for him, yet she was certain he would end their sham marriage soon now that his goal had been achieved.

She wrapped herself in a robe and moved to a window to look at the twinkling lights of Paris, knowing this wasn't the way to see or remember the city. How soon would he tell her they were through?

Sometimes she wished she had never met him. She rubbed her stomach, thinking about her baby. Matt was good with her little nieces and nephews. She had thought he would be around for a while for her baby.

She knew she needed to adjust and pick up and go on with her life, but Matt was dynamic and had swept into it, changing her world. He wasn't going to fade away or be forgotten easily.

She pulled her robe closer around her and closed her eyes, wanting sleep to come so she could stop worrying about her future.

"What are you doing, Brianna?" Matt asked, his deep voice a rumble in the dark room.

"Enjoying the city at night," she replied.

"I want you here in bed with me," he said sleepily. "I'm glad you like Paris," he added. "I can't work up the same enthusiasm."

"You miss a lot in life," she whispered, torn between annoyance that he was so totally focused on what he wanted and hurting because she had fallen in love with him in spite of it. She didn't receive an answer, but she went back to bed, slipping beneath the covers. He reached out and pulled her close against him, holding her tightly. For now, she held him, reassuring herself that she would be in his life a while longer.

The following afternoon, she shopped while Matt met with the investors and she was the first to arrive back at the hotel.

When he walked into the suite and tossed aside his topcoat, she knew he was in the group. Looking triumphant, he scooped her up into his embrace to kiss her passionately. "I'm in," he finally said. "We did it, Brianna. With thanks to you, who made this possible. I'll take you out for our own celebration tomorrow night, but tonight, they're taking us to a very expensive, very exclusive restaurant."

"Congratulations!" she said, wondering again how long their sham marriage would last now that the reason for it had vanished.

The evening should have been a warm memory in a restaurant with exotic French fare. She enjoyed sitting beside Signore Rufulli. All seemed happy to have her join them and everyone celebrated Matt becoming part of the group.

Flying home on Thursday, she had memories stored away, but along with them was the chilling knowledge that Matt no longer needed their union.

Before sunrise Friday morning, his cell phone rang and Matt stretched out a long arm, picking it up and flicking it open. He answered in a sensual, satisfied tone while she continued to run her fingers lightly over his chest and lower.

He listened such a long time she looked up. When she saw he was scowling, she guessed he was hearing bad news. Had a stock market somewhere in the world dropped during the night?

"How bad is it?" he asked quietly.

She rolled away and sat up to look at him, her curiosity growing.

"When did it happen?" he asked in a solemn voice and she wondered what calamity had transpired.

"How's he doing now?" Matt asked.

She wrapped her arms around herself and waited. It was worse than she'd imagined because someone was hurt and from Matt's tone, it was someone important to him.

"Thank God for that," he said, glancing at her and she wondered if he wanted privacy for his conversation. She grabbed a robe and slipped out of bed, leaving the room for a few minutes.

When she returned, he was propped in bed, still talking, but his voice sounded normal and he smiled over something. She let out her breath because it evidently wasn't too dreadful.

She had put on a red lace gown and, shedding her robe, she slipped beneath the covers and saw him watching her. He pushed away the sheet, but she immediately pulled it back and sat up cross-legged to stare at him, holding the sheet to her chin.

Finally, he broke the connection and looked at her. "Sorry to wake you with that call. It was Lance. My dad has had a heart attack."

"Oh, no! I take it he's doing better."

"Yes, he is. It was mild. He had chest pains and Mom took him to the E.R. From what I understand, Lance indicated there were changes in Dad's EKG and he had elevated enzymes. They want to keep him for observation, so he'll stay in the hospital for now. The prognosis is very good. Later this morning I can talk to Dad. In the meantime," he said, reaching out to pull on the sheet she grasped beneath her chin.

"Wait a minute!" she said, keeping the sheet waded tightly in her fist. "Aren't you going to Miami?"

"No. Lance said Dad's doing fine now and I don't need to come."

"You've got to go," she said, aghast that he was brushing aside his father's rush to the E.R. "Your father had a heart attack and you have a plane at your disposal. You can drop everything to do as you please."

"I need to work. There's no need for a trip to see him, Brianna," Matt restated patiently. "I'll see Dad at the next family gathering. In the meantime, there is someone I want to see," he said, reaching out again, but she scooted back quickly and pushed away his hand.

"Matt, that's the coldest attitude I've ever known. You go see your father."

"I'm all grown up now and have my own life and he's supposed to have a full recovery. It wasn't that serious."

"No wonder you don't want any children!" she snapped, staring at him intently.

He scowled at her. "Brianna, my dad is doing fine. There's no reason for me to go traipsing off to Florida to see him when he's okay."

"He's had a *heart attack*. He's older. My word, Matt, don't you care?"

"Of course I do, but I cut the apron strings when I left home for college. I don't go running home to them with every little thing, nor do they with me. We're not that kind of family."

"Well, thank heavens, mine is," she said, thinking how they all rallied around whenever there was a crisis. "We may not have money, but we love each other."

"I love my parents," he said patiently, but she could hear

the note of irritation in his voice and knew she was aggravating him, but she couldn't stop. His parents seemed warm and nice and had welcomed her into the family.

"Brianna, I am not going to Florida, so drop it," Matt said forcefully.

"You really don't have a heart, Matt," she said and left the room, going to the bathroom where she could shut him out. He didn't care about family, not his or anyone else's. He was nice and generous and giving to people as long as it didn't involve him too intensely and personally.

Her first assessment of him as heartless, in love only with money and perhaps himself, had been accurate. That's all he was about. She was in love with him and she couldn't stop loving him, but she knew it was time to move on. She had money now, enough to do as she pleased. What was the point in remaining with Matt? Their philosophies of life were poles apart. She wasn't going to change him, wasn't going to influence him. He knew what he wanted and went after it with a ruthless determination that shut out the rest of the world. And he really didn't care about anything else except success and the acquisition of wealth. She didn't even think he truly cared around the trappings of wealth or the power it gave him. He lived for the sheer accumulation of money.

It was a cold way to be and he would never love anyone in the fullest sense of the word. Nor would he be a good father. She knew he would shower a child with gifts and give a child some attention, but that all-accepting love that she already felt for her baby was something Matt could not attain. Nor did he want to.

He was selfish to the core and the sooner she moved on, the better off she would be. The cold realization hurt and tears stung her eyes. She thought about her future. If she stayed he would shower her with care throughout her pregnancy and childbirth. She knew he would be at her side for that—unless some crisis arose in his business. Then he'd be off and gone and return with presents for her to make up for his absence.

Did she want to give that up this early? Stay and enjoy his attention and help. It was tempting because it would be lonely and more difficult on her own even with money to buy whatever she wanted. Also, his very generous allowance would end if she walked away.

Yet the thought of making love to him had soured. Could she turn off her feelings about his coldness? She rubbed her neck, torn between going and staying, knowing she shouldn't rush into a decision she would regret later.

She recalled the night she'd met his parents and his father, Travis, saying to her, "I hope you'll bring him to see us. We don't see much of him, but I understand that better than his mother does." As far as Brianna was concerned, that meant that they'd like to see a lot more of their son than they did.

She heard a knock at the door and went to open it, looking up at Matt. Her heart thudded and for an instant, all her thoughts of leaving him vanished. How could she walk out when each time she saw him, she wanted to kiss him?

"Come in, Matt," she said, stepping back.

"I thought I'd see if you'd like to go downstairs with me to get something to eat. I think we were headed that way when we were interrupted by the telephone."

She nodded. "I'm going to shower. I'll be down shortly," she said, noticing his jeans and T-shirt and knowing she should shower and dress.

"Fine. See you downstairs. I'll get breakfast."

Closing the door, she waited for him to leave and then she stepped out to go to the closet, where she selected jeans and a blue sweater, got underwear and went to shower.

Downstairs she found him in the kitchen with egg casserole, ham, oatmeal and a platter of fruit on the table. He had orange juice and milk poured for her. While snow fell outside, they sat at the table near the fire. "If I go to Florida now, it's close enough to Thanksgiving that they'll want us both to come and stay."

"That wouldn't be the end of the world," she said, picking at her food and still thinking about her future, feeling cold and forlorn. "You can take some more time off."

"Look, if it would make you feel better about my dad, we can call Lance and you can talk to him."

She lowered her fork. "You don't get it. If your father was going to be released from the hospital tonight and go home and I could talk to him right now, I would. Or to put it another way—if this were my mom, I would be packing right now to go and I'd probably leave within the hour to see her. So talking to your brother really doesn't matter. I know your dad is going to survive this and I believe you when you say that the prognosis is good. But people are more important to me than money. You've always known that. Family is way more important than career."

"Brianna, you'd do anything short of a criminal act to get that degree. You wouldn't let your family interfere with you getting it and you didn't stay home with them. You moved to Laramie to get an education and you've stuck with it."

"I'd go home to see Mom if she had a heart attack," she replied, knowing she was being stubborn with him, but still aggravated by his cavalier attitude.

"Admirable, but in my case unnecessary. And I would understand if the situation were reversed."

"I recall your dad telling me that he was happy to see you marry and maybe now they would see more of you," Brianna replied.

"My dad said that?"

"Yes, he did."

"Mom I can understand. She would be happier if none of us had ever left home. She likes having us around, but we all grew up and moved on and it would have been odd if we hadn't."

Brianna turned to look at the fire and think about the coming week when he would be gone. She could take her time to contemplate her future and decide what she should do. She was tempted to tell him it was over now, but she knew that would be foolish. She had too much to gain by staying if she could get a better grip on her emotion and let go some of her affection for him.

They ate in silence until she thought she couldn't get down another bite. "Excuse me, Matt," she said, getting up and carrying her dishes to the sink to rinse them and put them in the dishwasher.

"You don't need to do that," he said.

"I know. It's habit and I don't mind." The room became silent again and she suspected their quasi-marriage was over.

"Dammit, Brianna, I'm not going and that's the end of the matter. Dad doesn't need me."

"Watch out, Matt. If you're not careful, someday, no one will need you," she said softly and one dark eyebrow arched.

"As long as I have a fortune, a lot of people will want and love me," he said in a cynical tone.

"Yes, that's true and you'll always know your fortune is exactly why." Her hurt deepened at his self-absorbed, callous attitude.

"I'm such an ogre?"

"Of course not. You're charming and irresistible in too many ways, and you'll always have women who love you and men who like you, so you'll never be lonely," she said, thinking all his relationships would be as shallow in the future as they had been in the past.

"Your arguments are contradictory," he stated, assessing her intently. "Someday you plan to be an attorney. You need to get your argument tight and to the point."

She smiled stiffly. "I'll remember that bit of advice. I know you'll find as much happiness in your future as you have in your past."

Something flickered in the depths of his eyes and a muscle worked in his jaw while he clenched his fists. "I'm not going to Florida. My dad doesn't need to see me, nor has he asked me to come."

"You've made that more than clear," she said and watched him turn and leave the room.

Tears threatened, but she fought shedding them, knowing they had been headed for this moment from the start, but never expecting it to hurt so badly.

In many ways she wanted to give his money back to him and walk away, feeling free from a bad bargain. Yet she knew that would be foolish and hurt not only herself, but her baby and her family. Too much was at stake, and Matt's money would secure the future for all of them. And he would never miss it because he had already amassed enormous wealth and was primarily engrossed in the acquisition of more, not the enjoyment of having it.

That day as she went about her exercise routine, she considered her decision. She loved Matt and she wanted to be with him, but it was ridiculous for her to stay and hope he'd someday change his basic nature. As much as it hurt, she wanted out of the fake marriage, wanted to tell the truth to her family, wanted to go on with her life. A life that had been transformed by Matt.

She knew he would protest and she was equally certain he wouldn't want her to go despite the temporary nature of the whole arrangement. And how much harder it would be to leave after the baby came. Yet that might be the time when Matt would have grown tired of them. So why wait until there were two hearts to break?

She had to get out of this fake marriage now.

Monday morning, she was determined to get up before he was out and gone so she could break the news to him that their marriage was over.

Matt had already showered and gone down to breakfast. She showered and dressed quickly, hurrying downstairs to catch him before he left.

She found him in his study, poring over papers in front of him at his desk. His suit jacket was tossed on a chair and he hadn't tightened his navy tie. A fire blazed in the fireplace and the crackle and pop of burning logs was the only sound in the room. In spite of her thick blue sweater and jeans, the heat from the flames was welcome. She was chilled to the bone.

"Knock, knock," she said as she entered and he looked up, tossing down his pen before he leaned back in his chair. "Matt, I want to talk to you," she said, crossing the room to stand by the fire. "I'll be brief. I know you have to go soon."

"Come in. You look upset. What's up?" he asked. He leaned back with his hands behind his head and his long legs stretched out in front of him.

"I've given thought to the future and to us," she said. "I guess it started when your father had his heart attack. We married with an agreement and we've both fulfilled our part of the bargain. I helped you get into the investors' group and you paid me the money you promised—part of it still due. Therefore this marriage has accomplished its purpose. It was never intended to be a permanent arrangement. Right?"

"Right," he said, lowering his hands and coming to his feet to rest his hands on his hips. Thick curls fell on his forehead and he was handsome, sexy and appealing. Her heart gave a twist, but this was inevitable. Better to get it done and over.

"When we discussed a marriage of convenience, I recall you saying that once you're invited into the investment group, you wouldn't hold me to two years. You told me that I can stay that long, but if I wanted out sooner, I could go."

"You're walking out?" he asked in disbelief, and for once, his total self-assurance looked shaken.

"Yes, I am," she answered, hurting and hoping she wouldn't cry in front of him. "I see no reason to stay longer. You've achieved your goal and got what you wanted. You're through with me—"

"Not really, Brianna. We have a good thing going here—and you've acted like you thought it was great."

"The physical relationship between us is fine, but my emotions are tangled up in it. I haven't had enough relationships to make comparisons. It's been wonderful, Matt, and you know it, but it's time to go. Look how distant you are with your blood relatives. If I stay, I'll fall in love with you and then it'll be the same way with me and with the baby."

"I can't believe you want to do this."

She ran her hand across her cheek. "Thanks to you, I have sufficient money to live comfortably and provide for my baby. My family will be with me for the baby's birth. I find it difficult to imagine you being interested in a baby or wanting to go through this pregnancy with me."

"I think you're jumping to conclusions," he said quietly. "I don't want you to go," he said, walking closer.

"All we're having is an affair. A legally contracted affair. It isn't a real marriage and you never intended it to be," she said softly as if she were explaining something to a child. Tears still threatened, and she swiped her eyes again as she gazed up at him.

"You don't even want to go—"

"Of course I don't want to go!" she cried, finally losing her control. "I'm probably in love with you and even though you're charming and sex is the best, there's no future here. I don't want to end up like Nicole, dragging around after you and trying to recapture your attention."

"That's entirely different. You're unique and maybe we'll both fall in love. Isn't that worth waiting to let happen?"

"Maybe? *Maybe?* No. I think I'll get hurt worse and I don't want to have all the upheaval of moving when I have an infant to care for. It'll be much easier now to find a place, get settled and get ready for my baby."

Closing the distance between them, he wrapped his arms around her and kissed her for a long time. As she remaining stiffly in his arms, her resistance melted until she responded, aware of the salty taste of her tears.

He raised his head, wiping away her tears with his thumbs. "Don't cry. Stay with me. We're happy together and have a good thing going. If it makes you feel better about it, I'll promise to keep this marriage together for the full two years and then you won't be so worried about the future. How's that?"

She shook her head. "Not enough. I guess you made me want it all, Matt. I want a real marriage and if I can't have a real one, I don't want one at all."

His eyes darkened and he clamped his jaw closed. "There's not going to be a real marriage. You've known that from the start."

"Yes, you've made it abundantly clear," she replied, gazing steadily into his eyes.

"You know what you want. I'm not going to stick around and argue. If you want out, you're free to go," he said and the words cut with the sharpness of a knife. "I'll help you move any way I can and do what I can for you about the baby. I'll still pay for nannies when the time comes. We should part friends, Brianna."

"Thank you," she said quietly, once again fighting to keep from crying.

"You can call me whenever you want anything." He slipped his hand behind her head to caress her nape, moving closer again. "If you change your mind, let me know. I'll welcome you back into my life—anytime in the near future."

He looked handsome, appealing, as irresistible as ever and she wanted him to tell her to stay and let it be a real marriage.

Instead, they stared silently at each other, each one wanting something different, each one with conflicting desires that were impossible to resolve. Suddenly, he pulled her into his arms again for another passionate kiss.

Leaning over her, he held her tightly while his tongue thrust deeply into her mouth and he kissed her long and thoroughly.

Her heart thudded and she clung to him, kissing him in return, knowing this was his goodbye. She ran her hand across his broad shoulders that felt warm through the thin cotton of his shirt. She was tempted beyond measure to cry out that she would stay and take her chances on the future with him. She didn't want to go. She loved him and might forever.

Finally, she pushed against him. He released her only a fraction. Breathing hard, he gazed at her. "Don't go," he said.

"I love you," she whispered and he flinched. The gesture was harsh and cut as much as his words had. He shifted away a few inches, tucking her hair behind her ear.

"I can't do the permanent marriage, Brianna. I'm not into long relationships, much less a lifetime commitment. You've known that from the first night."

"I know. Saying that it's been wonderful sounds woefully inadequate for all you've done. I hope you make back your investment and oodles more. May you make another billion or so, Matt." She slipped her arm around his neck and kissed him again, long, heated and final. When she drew away, she was crying.

"Don't pay the rest of the money you and I agreed on. There's enough invested to take care of me, my baby and my family sufficiently. We have a fortune now."

"Don't be ridiculous. We have an agreement—a written contract. You've lived up to your part of the bargain."

"If you give me more, I'll send it to charities."

"That's foolish, Brianna," he stated. "Spend the money on yourself and your family. With a child to raise, you can use it. Charity begins at home."

"So does love, Matt," she said solemnly. "You're missing what's important in life."

"I'm not certain you would have made that statement when you first met me. With a couple of million, your perspective has changed."

"Not my basic feelings about family and love."

"Remember, you can change your mind about this. All you have to do is let me know," he said.

"This is officially goodbye," she said, hoping she could be out of his house when he returned from his New York trip.

"Sure. But I intend to keep in touch."

She nodded, letting him think what he wanted. He gave her a long, hard study and then turned to pick up his jacket and leave, closing the door behind him.

"Goodbye," she whispered again. She had no intention of turning into another Nicole, someone pursuing him when he didn't want to be pursued.

Shaking and cold, she walked to the fire to warm her icy hands, knowing flames probably couldn't remove the chill that enveloped her. Matt had gone out of her life. Would she ever stop loving him? How long before he replaced her and forgot her?

She suspected it wouldn't take him long at all. All

week he would be taken up with business and making more money.

When she entered her enormous closet and looked at the array of clothes she now owned—a mink coat, designer dresses and shoes, purses that at one time would have paid her rent for months—she had another pang for the life she was tossing aside.

She would need help moving her belongings. Her brothers and brothers-in-law could do it without difficulty. The first and most important thing was to find somewhere to live. The next thing was to let her family know that she was leaving Matt.

She wanted out of Matt's house immediately and finding a comfortable hotel suite became top priority. Wiping her eyes, she went to the computer to check out hotels.

Since Laramie was where all her family would be, she thought about looking there later for a house. Melody had already purchased a house and was moving in another week.

Brianna got down the one small suitcase she'd brought when she'd moved in with Matt. Now she owned so much it would take an entire set of luggage and probably more than one trunk. She wanted him home and in his arms and their lives together to go on the way they had. This time when tears came, she gave vent to them, leaning against the doorjamb and crying, knowing it was over with Matt.

Matt immersed himself in business and stayed busy every night in New York. Even so, he couldn't get

Brianna out of his thoughts. Occasionally he would spot a tall, leggy woman with black hair like hers, and his heart would skip a beat.

Too well, he remembered being there with her and the first time she had seen Saint Patrick's, her first trip to Central Park. He saw her too many places, too often, and he couldn't shake thinking about her.

He called her each night, but she never answered. For the first time he realized she really might be gone out of his life completely. She wasn't predictable or like any other woman he'd ever known. If she wanted to vanish out of his life, she would. He was sure he could track her down, but as far as seeing her socially or even taking her out again, he faced the fact that might be impossible now.

The realization she had really cut all ties hurt. He'd had her final check deposited into her account at the bank and he expected he would hear from her about it. Matt wondered if Brianna would ask his suggestions about investing the money. Or would she stick to what she'd said and give her final payment to charity? He couldn't imagine her doing any such thing.

Wednesday evening his cell phone rang and he answered instantly, hope flaring that he would hear Brianna's voice.

Instead, it was one of the investors discussing an opportunity that had arisen. Matt's attention was taken by the prospect and he worked into late hours, sleeping little and getting up to check on the market.

By Friday, he had made over a million from the investment. That night in the hotel he wrote down the figures, staring at them. For the first time the return gave him no great satisfaction. What he really wanted was Brianna in his life—even more than money. The realization shocked him, and he wondered when she had become so damn important to him that everything else diminished.

Had she been right that money wasn't the all-important facet of life, less meaningful than love? He couldn't answer his own question except for that in this case, he would have given not only the million but more to have her with him again.

He'd never thought anything could be as great as the accumulation of wealth, the challenge and success of making a big deal, but now it wasn't his prime need. He had a huge fortune. Even the bet with his cousins had lost its priority.

Disgusted with life and with himself, he pushed away and paced the room impatiently. He strode to the window to look out over the city. Lights sparkled in every direction. What was she doing now?

He missed Brianna and her exuberance and enthusiasm. She was a good listener and he'd grown accustomed to talking freely to her about business—something he didn't feel would be wise to do with anyone else, even Zach. He wondered if she'd ever know that he'd taken her suggestion about investing more of himself into Cheyenne. Now he wished he had told her that he'd asked Zach to check into some particular properties.

Matt knew he'd get accustomed to life without her, just as he always had after a breakup, but at present, it bothered him.

Turning to his usual solution after a breakup, he intended to immerse himself in work. Tomorrow, Saturday morning, he would fly to London and work there all next week.

Late Thursday he returned home, where he worked until he fell asleep over his desk before he finally went to bed. He was exhausted, yet still unable to sleep peacefully, dreaming about Brianna and waking to want her in his arms.

It jolted him the following week when he received the first thank-you from a nonprofit literacy group. Any donations he made went through the foundation set up in his name. He realized this was Brianna's doing, and she was giving the last payment to charity just as she had said she would.

Staring at the note in his hand, he stood a long time wondering about her and the depth of her feelings. He hadn't really thought she would turn down his money under any circumstances. Had she done this to emphasize to him that love was more important and he was far too material?

He spent long hours at his office and exercised several hours each day, but nothing filled the emptiness he felt. He hated missing her and reassured himself that with time his longing would fade away.

One night in his office at home, he sat thinking about

Brianna. He missed her dreadfully and he'd never missed anyone before. She had changed his life and he couldn't get his old life back. She was everywhere he looked, yet not really there, only a phantom of a memory. He missed her and wanted her and realized he had fallen in love with her, something he had never expected to have happen. Through affairs and friendships, women had been secondary in his life. Even his family had always faded to the background, but Brianna wouldn't fade away or diminish or get out of his thoughts.

He began to wonder if her family was settled in Laramie, going to school as they had planned and if she had moved there to be near them.

He'd been to the steak house where he'd first found her, but no one there had seen her. He knew he could hire someone to find her, but there wasn't much point in it. Unless he wanted to make a permanent commitment. Wouldn't that be far better than this hellish misery he was going through constantly?

Brianna tried to keep her mind on the booklet in front of her. She was trying to decide on courses for the spring semester at the University of Wyoming. She sat at a desk, poring over brochures and selecting classes, trying to get a schedule that would work. Because of her marriage to Matt, she would be behind schedule now on graduating, but only by a semester. She wanted to make certain she got her degree and she knew the baby would throw her timetable into upheaval.

Now because of Matt, she would have all the help she

wanted to hire and her mother lived here in Laramie and would be available and eager to help.

Her thoughts wandered to Matt. She missed him more than ever and wondered how long it would take her to get over him and to stop thinking about him constantly. She was lonely, hurting and missing his vitality and loving.

She had told her mother everything about her marriage and agreement with Matt.

There were moments she wished she had stayed until he walked out on her, but she knew she was better off making the break now.

She finally talked to a counselor about the courses she wanted to take and left to return to the sprawling condo she had purchased in a gated area that was in a relatively new area of Laramie.

When she turned onto her street, she saw a sleek black car parked in front of her house. As she turned into her drive, she wondered whose it was. Glancing over her shoulder, she saw Matt step out of the car.

Her heart missed a beat. He looked handsome in a leather jacket, jeans, western boots and a wide-brimmed Stetson. She stopped her car and climbed out to go meet him while her racing heart speeded even faster.

"What are you doing here?" she asked, watching him approach, snow crunching beneath his boots.

Nine

He walked up to her and she threw her arms around his neck at the same time he pulled her into his embrace. And then he kissed her.

Holding him tightly and forgetting all her resolutions, she wanted him more than ever.

She longed to push away his thick coat and heavy clothes to run her hands all over him. She kissed him hungrily while Matt tightened his arms around her.

He picked her up. "Door key?" he asked and then kissed her before she could answer him.

He held her while she unlocked the door and then carried her in, kicking the door shut behind him.

"Why are you here?" she asked, refusing to think about telling him goodbye all over again.

"I missed you," he said, glancing beyond her. "Where's your bedroom?"

She pointed as he kissed her again while he walked where she had directed.

An hour later she stirred in his arms as he rolled on his side and propped his head on his hand to look at her.

"I wasn't going to do this," she said quietly, gazing up at him solemnly and brushing his jaw lightly with the tips of her fingers as if to reassure herself that he was real.

"I wasn't, either. I've tried every way I could think of to forget you."

"Every way?" she asked, wondering if there had been a woman in his life.

"Maybe not every way," he said in a husky voice. "I want you back. What do I have to do? We're already married."

"Not really," she answered. "That's a technicality and our contract was for two years only."

"Will you marry me for real?"

Her heart missed a beat as she gazed up into his blue eyes. "Is that a proposal?"

"It is. I'm asking you to be my wife now and forever. I don't like being without you. I think about you constantly and miss you all the time and I don't want to go on like this."

"Do you mean it?" she asked, sitting up and tugging up the sheet beneath her chin.

"Will you marry me?"

"Forever?" she cried.

"Forever," he stated emphatically.

"Yes! Of course I will. I already have. I love you!"

"Darlin', I love you."

"More than money?" she asked, squinting her eyes and looking intently at him.

"Much more than money," he mused. "I found out that you were right about so many things, particularly what's really vital. Now let me see. What advantages are there to you over money? Soft, curvaceous, best kisser on earth, sexiest woman, a necessity for me to exist and function. Should we have another wedding?"

"I don't think so. Just another honeymoon."

"I'll vote for that one," he said. "You name where you want to go and I'll take you for as long as you want. I'll do anything to keep you happy."

She brushed his thick black curls away from his forehead and let her fingers slide down his cheek and along his jaw, feeling the faint stubble. "I didn't think you'd ever be back."

"I didn't, either. It was as big a surprise to me as to you to find out that I can't get along without you," he said solemnly and she smiled.

"I'm glad. I wasn't doing so well myself."

"Speaking of how you're doing. You still don't look pregnant. Are you sure you didn't make all that up?"

"Absolutely. I've been to see the doctor and I'm fine. I don't show yet and I guess part of it is because I'm tall. I don't know. He said everything is okay. I'll get bigger sometime so enjoy my skinny looks now."

"I intend to. Every way possible."

She held his jaw. "What about the baby? Do you mind?"

"I'll adopt the baby and it'll be mine. This baby will know me as its daddy. A daddy who loves it very much."

"Do you care whether I have a girl or boy?"

"Nope. As long as everyone is healthy and if you're happy, I'm happy."

They gazed into each other's eyes and she smiled at him, joy bursting in her. "I can't believe you're here and I'm so happy you are."

"I love you, Brianna, love you with all my heart."

She turned to kiss him, pausing to look up at him. "I never thought I'd hear you say that."

"I love you, darlin'," he said. "My wife. Decide where you want to go for a real honeymoon."

"Anywhere with you will be paradise," she said, pulling him closer to kiss him.

Epilogue

The following October...

"Bye, Mom, thanks," Brianna said, completing her call home to her mother. "Matt, will you stop a minute!"

He chuckled as he nuzzled her neck and she turned in his arms to hug him. "Let me talk on the phone, for heaven's sake!"

"All I was doing was holding you and kissing you a very little bit," he said innocently. "How's Jenna?"

"Jenna is fine and Mom is having a wonderful time with her and my sisters are there now so everyone is happy." She held up the baby's picture and they both looked at it.

"Brianna, I'll swear if I didn't know better, I'd think

this is my own flesh and blood. She's got my black curly hair and my blue eyes."

"Indeed, she does, but she also looks like me," Brianna said, smiling at him and looking back at their daughter. "She's beautiful. It was wonderful of your cousins to put off this weekend until Jenna was a couple of months old."

"We're great guys," he declared smugly and she laughed. She glanced around their large bedroom with bamboo furniture and plank floors. A ceiling fan turned lazily overhead. "This is really grand, but only because you're here," she said. Her smile faded as she gazed up at him. "Thank you for getting out of your investors' group so you'd be home more."

"You were right about what's important in life. And I'm glad you postponed law school indefinitely."

She kissed him lightly. "We have enough money for a good life in Cheyenne."

"That's a little bit of an understatement," he remarked dryly. "But it is good, and so was spending a week with my folks last month."

"Speaking of spending time with someone—it's past when we were supposed to join the others for the dinner party. We're already twenty minutes late," she said, glancing at her watch.

"They won't care," he said, continuing to nuzzle her throat and shower kisses on her temple and ear.

"I care. Now come on and let's join them."

"Sure," he said, straightening up and watching her cross the room. "You barely ever looked pregnant and now no one can guess by appearance that you had a baby a few months back. You look gorgeous."

She glanced in the mirror. "Thank you. You look good yourself," she said. "C'mon, Matt, and we'll go see your friends."

He groaned. "And listen to Chase crow over winning this bet."

"That's what you get for making such an extravagant bet," she said as he caught her hand and they left their island house for the large community building they all shared. Music carried on the night air from the band and outside flames danced beneath the grilling meat being turned by a cook.

Holding her hand, he led her up the steps into the large open room where a band played and the others danced.

The music ended and Brianna and Matt joined the other two couples. Brianna felt lucky to be Matt's wife and to be included in this group. From the first moment she met them, both Laurel and Megan had been friendly. Their handsome husbands had been, also.

"Finally, the newlyweds join us. A waiter should come by with drinks," Chase said.

The music commenced and Matt turned to take her into his arms to dance as the other couples paired off to dance.

Later in the evening the women sat in a cluster while the men stood nearby.

"This is a wonderful weekend," Brianna said.

"Wonderful and wacky," Megan added, "with their crazy bet, but it got us all together and that's good."

"They'll think up some new scheme," Laurel stated.

"I guess we can be glad for that bet though. I think that's what got us all together with our husbands. Right?"

"You're right," Megan said.

"What's happening?" Matt came up to join them and pulled a chair close to Brianna while the other men came to sit by their wives.

Matt raised his glass in a toast. "Here's to the winner of the bet—Chase. I never thought you'd win," Matt said. "I have to tell you."

"My oil beat out your investments and your businesses," Chase said, smiling at his cousins.

After a slight cheer, they all touched glasses and sipped their drinks.

"We were thinking about another possible bet this next year—" Jared began, but the women shouted and finally he looked at his cousins and threw up his hands.

"No more wild bets!" Megan declared, and they all laughed.

The band commenced playing again and Matt asked Brianna to dance. He wrapped his arms around her to dance slowly. "I love you, darlin'. My life is complete with you in it."

"Chase rented this island for the weekend and all this came with it?"

"Not all. The winner had to take care of the weekend, so this is Chase's deal. It's been fun, but I'm ready to go back to our own place. I want you to myself."

He waved to his cousins as they left and in minutes they were in the privacy of their bedroom, where Matt drew her into his embrace. "I love you with all my heart."

She pulled him closer to kiss him, holding him tightly, filled with love and joy for the man she would adore always.

* * * * *

*Celebrate 60 years of pure reading pleasure with
Harlequin®!*

*Harlequin Presents® is proud to introduce its
gripping new miniseries,*
THE ROYAL HOUSE OF KAREDES.
*An exquisite coronation diamond, split as a symbol of
a warring royal family's feud, is missing! But
whoever reunites the diamond halves will rule all....*

*Welcome to eight brand-new titles that unfold to
reveal the stories of kings and queens, princes and
princesses torn apart by pride and power, but finally
reunited by love.*

*Step into the world of Karedes with
BILLIONAIRE PRINCE, PREGNANT MISTRESS
Available July 2009 from Harlequin Presents®.*

ALEXANDROS KAREDES, snow dusting the shoulders of his leather jacket and glittering like jewels in his dark hair, stood at the door. Maria felt the blood drain from her head.

"Good evening, Ms. Santos."

His voice was as she remembered it. Deep. Husky. Perfect English, but with the faintest hint of a Greek accent. And cold, as cold as it had been that awful morning she would never forget, when he'd accused her of horrible things, called her terrible names....

"Aren't you going to ask me in?"

She fought for composure. Last time they'd faced each other, they'd been on his turf. Now they were on hers. She was in command here, and that meant everything.

"There's a sign on the door downstairs," she said, her

tone every bit as frigid as his. "It says, 'No soliciting or vagrants.'"

His lips drew back in a wolfish grin. "Very amusing."

"What do you want, Prince Alexandros?"

A tight smile eased across his mouth and it killed her that even now, knowing he was a vicious, arrogant man, she couldn't help but notice what a handsome mouth it was. Chiseled. Generous. Beautiful, like the rest of him, which made him living proof that beauty could, indeed, be only skin deep.

"Such formality, Maria. You were hardly so proper the last time we were together."

She knew his choice of words was deliberate. She felt her face heat; she couldn't help that but she damned well didn't have to let him lure her into a verbal sparring match.

"I'll ask you once more, your highness. What do you want?"

"Ask me in and I'll tell you."

"I have no intention of asking you in. Tell me why you're here or don't. It's your choice, just as it will be my choice to shut the door in your face."

He laughed. It infuriated her but she could hardly blame him. He was tall—six-two, six-three—and though he stood with one shoulder leaning against the door frame, hands tucked casually into the pockets of the jacket, his pose was deceptive. He was strong, with the leanly muscled body of a well-trained athlete.

She remembered his body with painful clarity. The feel of him under her hands. The power of him moving over her. The taste of him on her tongue.

Suddenly, he straightened, his laughter gone. "I have not come this distance to stand in your doorway," he said coldly, "and I am not going to leave until I am ready to do so. I suggest you stand aside and stop behaving like a petulant child."

A petulant child? Was that what he thought? This man who had spent hours making love to her and had then accused her of—of trading her body for profit?

Except it had not been love, it had been sex. And the sooner she got rid of him, the better.

She let go of the doorknob and stepped aside. "You have five minutes."

He strolled past her, bringing cold air and the scent of the night with him. She swung toward him, arms folded. He reached past her, pushed the door closed, then folded his arms, too. She wanted to open the door again but she'd be damned if she was going to get into a who's-in-charge-here argument with him. She was in charge, and he would surely see a tussle over the ground rules as a sign of weakness.

Instead, she looked past him at the big clock above her work table.

"Ten seconds gone," she said briskly. "You're wasting time, your highness."

"What I have to say will take longer than five minutes."

"Then you'll just have to learn to economize. More than five minutes, I'll call the police."

Instantly, his hand was wrapped around her wrist. He tugged her toward him, his dark-chocolate eyes almost black with anger.

"You do that and I'll tell every tabloid shark I can contact about how Maria Santos tried to buy a five-hundred-thousand-dollar commission by seducing a prince." He smiled thinly. "They'll lap it up."

* * * * *

What will it take for this billionaire prince to realize
he's falling in love with his mistress…?
Look for
BILLIONAIRE PRINCE, PREGNANT MISTRESS
by Sandra Marton.
Available July 2009
from Harlequin Presents®.

We'll be spotlighting a different series every month
throughout 2009 to celebrate our 60th anniversary.

Look for Harlequin® Presents in July!

TWO CROWNS, TWO ISLANDS, ONE LEGACY
A royal family, torn apart by pride and its lust for
power, reunited by purity and passion

Step into the world of Karedes
beginning this July with

BILLIONAIRE PRINCE,
PREGNANT MISTRESS
by
Sandra Marton

Eight volumes to collect and treasure!

THE BELLES OF TEXAS

They're as strong as the state that raised them. The Belle sisters aren't afraid to go after what they want, whether it's reclaiming their ranch or their family.

Linda Warren
CAITLYN'S PRIZE

Thanks to her deceased father's gambling debts, Caitlyn Belle's beloved High Five Ranch is in dire straits. Particularly because the will stipulates that if the ranch doesn't turn a profit in six months, it must be sold to Judd Calhoun—the man Caitlyn jilted fourteen years ago. And Cait knows Judd has been waiting a long time for his revenge....

*Look for the first book
in The Belles of Texas miniseries,
on sale in July wherever books are sold.*

What's a **STEELE** to do when he comes home to find
a beautiful woman asleep in his bed?

NEW YORK TIMES BESTSELLING AUTHOR
BRENDA JACKSON

Playboy Donovan Steele has
one goal: to make sultry
Natalie Ford his latest conquest.
She's resisting, but their
sizzling chemistry makes her
think twice. Once she reveals
her true identity, will Donovan
disappear—for good?

On sale JUNE 30, 2009
wherever books are sold.

**Indulge in the latest Forged of Steele novel, the
anticipated follow-up to IRRESISTIBLE FORCES.**

KIMANI
ROMANCE

You're invited to join our Tell Harlequin Reader Panel!

By joining our new reader panel you will:

- Receive Harlequin® books—they are FREE and yours to keep with no obligation to purchase anything!
- Participate in fun online surveys
- Exchange opinions and ideas with women just like you
- Have a say in our new book ideas and help us publish the best in women's fiction

In addition, you will have a chance to win great prizes and receive special gifts!
See Web site for details. Some conditions apply.
Space is limited.

To join, visit us at
www.TellHarlequin.com.

REQUEST YOUR FREE BOOKS!

2 FREE NOVELS
PLUS 2
FREE GIFTS!

Silhouette® Desire®

Passionate, Powerful, Provocative!

YES! Please send me 2 FREE Silhouette Desire® novels and my 2 FREE gifts (gifts are worth about $10). After receiving them, if I don't wish to receive any more books, I can return the shipping statement marked "cancel". If I don't cancel, I will receive 6 brand-new novels every month and be billed just $4.05 per book in the U.S. or $4.74 per book in Canada. That's a savings of almost 15% off the cover price! It's quite a bargain! Shipping and handling is just 50¢ per book.* I understand that accepting the 2 free books and gifts places me under no obligation to buy anything. I can always return a shipment and cancel at any time. Even if I never buy another book, the two free books and gifts are mine to keep forever.   225 SDN EYMS 326 SDN EYM4

Name   (PLEASE PRINT)

Address   Apt. #

City   State/Prov.   Zip/Postal Code

Signature (if under 18, a parent or guardian must sign)

Mail to the Silhouette Reader Service:
IN U.S.A.: P.O. Box 1867, Buffalo, NY 14240-1867
IN CANADA: P.O. Box 609, Fort Erie, Ontario L2A 5X3

Not valid to current subscribers of Silhouette Desire books.

Want to try two free books from another line?
Call 1-800-873-8635 or visit www.morefreebooks.com.

* Terms and prices subject to change without notice. Prices do not include applicable taxes. Sales tax applicable in N.Y. Canadian residents will be charged applicable provincial taxes and GST. Offer not valid in Quebec. This offer is limited to one order per household. All orders subject to approval. Credit or debit balances in a customer's account(s) may be offset by any other outstanding balance owed by or to the customer. Please allow 4 to 6 weeks for delivery. Offer available while quantities last.

Your Privacy: Silhouette Books is committed to protecting your privacy. Our Privacy Policy is available online at www.eHarlequin.com or upon request from the Reader Service. From time to time we make our lists of customers available to reputable third parties who may have a product or service of interest to you. If you would prefer we not share your name and address, please check here. ☐

SDES09R

In 2009 Harlequin celebrates
60 years of pure reading pleasure!

We're marking this occasion by offering
16 **FREE** full books to download and read.

Visit
www.HarlequinCelebrates.com
to choose from a variety of
great romance stories
that are absolutely **FREE!**

(Total approximate retail value of $60)

We invite you to visit and share the Web site
with your friends, family
and anyone who enjoys reading.

COMING NEXT MONTH
Available July 14, 2009

#1951 ROYAL SEDUCER—Michelle Celmer
Man of the Month
The prince thought his bride-to-be knew their marriage was only a diplomatic arrangement. But their passion in the bedroom tells a different story....

#1952 TAMING THE TEXAS TYCOON—
Katherine Garbera
Texas Cattleman's Club: Maverick County Millionaires
Seducing his secretary wasn't part of the plan—yet now he'll never be satisfied with just one night.

#1953 INHERITED: ONE CHILD—Day Leclaire
Billionaires and Babies
Forced to marry to keep his niece, this billionaire finds the perfect solution in his very attractive nanny...until a secret she's harboring threatens to destroy everything.

#1954 THE ILLEGITIMATE KING—Olivia Gates
The Castaldini Crown
This potential heir will only take the crown on one condition— he'll take the king's daughter with it!

#1955 MAGNATE'S MAKE-BELIEVE MISTRESS—
Bronwyn Jameson
Secretly determined to expose his housekeeper's lies, he makes her his mistress to keep her close. But little does he know that he has the wrong sister!

#1956 HAVING THE BILLIONAIRE'S BABY—
Sandra Hyatt
After one hot night with his sister's enemy, he's stunned when she reveals she's carrying his baby!